MACLAY DAYS

MACLAY DAYS

stories • from • Glasgow

Lorn Macintyre

ARGYLL✠PUBLISHING

© Lorn Macintyre 2010

First published in 2010 by
Argyll Publishing
Glendaruel
Argyll PA22 3AE
Scotland
www.argyllpublishing.com

The author has asserted his moral rights.

**British Library Cataloguing-in-Publication Data.
A catalogue record for this book is available from
the British Library.**

ISBN 978 1 906134 62 4

Printing: JF Print Ltd., Sparkford, Somerset

To dearest Mary,
for all the years of support and unshakeable belief

ACKNOWLEDGEMENTS

To my friend Kenneth Fraser, for his recollections of Maclay Hall and for his help with research over the years.

To the archivists at the University of Glasgow and to the staff of the Glasgow Room, the Mitchell Library, Glasgow for their expertise.

To Lex Keith, bandleader, for his memories of playing in the St Andrew's Halls, Glasgow.

1. Pilgrimage

When Dr Murdo Maclean retired from his west coast of Scotland practice at the age of 65, his appreciative patients presented him with a pair of quality binoculars at a ceilidh in the village hall. He was a keen bird watcher and kept a telescope on a tripod at the picture window of the house he had built overlooking the bay where his yacht was anchored. When he saw an ivory gull sitting on the water one winter's day he booted up his computer and put it on Birdline. It was a mistake, because a hundred twitchers arrived in cars and on motor cycles and disrupted the peace of his habitation.

'We should go somewhere to celebrate,' his wife suggested a month or so before he saw his last patient.

'I'd like to go to Glasgow,' he told her as he was eating the mackerel that one of his patients had left in a pail at the back door.

'Glasgow? For goodness sake, Murdo, I'm talking about a proper trip abroad.'

'I'd like to go to Glasgow for old time's sake.'

'What does that mean?'

'I'd like to revisit the haunts of my university days in Glasgow.'

'You're a romantic, Murdo, but you're in for a shock. Glasgow will have changed a great deal. You're going to be disappointed.'

'I'll take my chance.'

'So when and what should I book for us?' she asked.

'Don't book anywhere. I'll go by myself for a couple of days and you can book us a holiday in France.'

He spent an afternoon surfing the web, finding the nearest hotel to Kelvingrove Park in Glasgow, and paid for two nights by credit card.

He didn't like driving long distances any more, so he took the train, treating himself to a first class seat, which meant that he received coffee, a newspaper and constant smiles from the attendant. For the previous Christmas his son Archie had given him an iPod. The doctor didn't think he could master the dinky silver instrument that was the size of a heart pacemaker and which could, apparently, hold several thousand tunes. But he had persevered at using the computer in his surgery, because the Health Board had decreed that written record cards were obsolete. From now on everything was to be online. In the last year of his practice he was able to bring up on the screen x-ray images that had been taken in the infirmary a hundred miles away, to swivel the screen to show his patient who smoked forty cigarettes a day what he had done to his lungs.

However, Murdo had managed to download a hundred

tunes by Scottish dance bands – reels, jigs and strathspeys – because at the age of ten he started a love affair with the accordion. He provided the music for the Scottish Country dance class which met each week in the village hall. The teacher, Miss Macdonald, would say deferentially: 'May I have sixteen bars please, Dr Maclean?' and he would oblige, watching his patients mastering the clover-leaf reels in Mairi's Wedding. Murdo Maclean had never confided his secret regret even to his wife: he would have preferred to have been a dance band leader than a doctor. Not that medicine hadn't had its rewards, but there wasn't the same thrill in fitting a stethoscope into one's ears as there was in sliding one's hands under the straps of an accordion. Oh certainly, there were new procedures, new drugs to dispense, and therefore new hope, but that couldn't compare with playing a new tune – especially one you had composed yourself. Murdo couldn't form a dance band in his practice because he was unable to travel any distance in the days before mobile phones, since his was a single practice in a wide area, and he had to be accessible at short notice to the farmer collapsing with a massive stroke.

The selection of tunes coming through the iPod plugs in his ears sent the physician to sleep as the train rocked him gently towards the city. He found himself dreaming more as he aged, the scenes regressing to his upbringing on the island where his father Archie had been the eccentric bank manager who preferred to sit in his office for most of the day, listening to old folks (who hadn't a penny in his bank, or a tooth of their own in their mouths) telling stories in impeccable Gaelic of worthies of the town and the strange experiences they had

had, such as seeing the funeral of an apparently hale and hearty man who was scything the next croft, but who would collapse the following week. Murdo had been inspired to learn the accordion as he came down the brae from school and heard Alasdair MacTavish composing a tune in the Ceilidh Bar before it opened for the evening's brisk business. He asked for a box for his twelfth birthday, and when he opened the case he was struck by the beauty of the red button-key melodeon. Within the week he could play a Gaelic tune and was sent for lessons to Mrs Mackenzie the music teacher, and within a year he was appearing on a platform in a ceilidh with Alasdair MacTavish.

When he went to the mainland to complete his school education he took his box with him, to play in the hostel, and brought it home at the weekends.

'You're spending too much time at that accordion,' his mother Alice rebuked him. 'You need to concentrate on your school work, to make something of your life.'

'His report cards are good,' Archie reminded his wife.

'Yes, but it said on the last one that he could do even better. You're going to have to put that accordion away if you want to be a doctor.'

But Murdo knew that playing the accordion in the school hostel in the evenings not only entertained his fellow residents, but also relaxed him and made the absorption of chemical formulae easier. Not only did he get sufficient Highers to get into medicine: he also was awarded the dux medal and an armful of prizes. His mother wanted him to go to St Andrews, away from the temptations of the city, but Murdo had set his heart on Glasgow because Alasdair

MacTavish had told him of the many opportunities for accordion players, since there were so many Highland associations which held regular dances and ceilidhs.

Alice relented, but insisted that he was to go into a hall of residence in Glasgow and not into a flat with other students. She accompanied him to the city to inspect the university's Maclay Hall in elegant Park Terrace overlooking Kelvingrove Park. She tested window ledges for dust with her gloved finger and lifted toilet seat covers. She also enquired about the wholesomeness of the food and was assured that porridge was served, as well as fish.

Murdo wakened when the train was running beside the Firth of Clyde. He regretted not having brought his presentation binoculars because of the birds out on the mud flats, but the train was going too fast for careful identification even with the best magnification. He remembered that he had spent one summer of his vacation playing in a band on the deck of an excursion steamer which left Glasgow in the early morning and beat down the Clyde coastal resorts. He had loved the experience of the sun in his face, playing reels as the steamer passed through the Kyles of Bute, and when they returned to the Broomielaw out of a spectacular sunset there would be a substantial sum to share out in the cap that the band leader had passed round.

The train hit the buffers in Queen Street Station and the doors jerked open. As Murdo wheeled off his suitcase he remembered arriving in the long-since demolished Buchanan Street Station in a steam train with straps on the windows, moquette seats in the compartments and pastel images of holiday destinations under the mesh of the rack. He had been invited to reunions of his medical year, but hadn't come to Glasgow because he would have had to find a locum for his practice. When the university's alumni magazine arrived, he didn't look at the death notices because he didn't want to be reminded of his own mortality by reading about classmates who had passed away.

Dr Maclean took a taxi to the Acorn Hotel, where he had asked for a room overlooking Kelvingrove Park. Half an hour later, when his clothes were hanging in the wardrobe, his razor on the shelf in the bathroom, his heart pills on the pillow as a reminder to take them at bedtime, he was walking up the path to Maclay Hall.

There had been over one hundred male students in the hall, but only fourteen single rooms. Murdo had shared with Donald Gunn, a divinity and Celtic student from the far north who never seemed to smile and who had a stutter. When he saw Murdo lifting his accordion out of its case he asked him why he had brought it to university.

'To play it of course. Would you like a tune now?'

'I wi-would not,' was the indignant reply.

'Why not?'

'Because it's an instrument of the devil.'

Murdo took out his pack of Capstan, slid it open and offered his roommate a smoke, but he shook his head vigorously.

'Smoking's bad for you. It corrodes the lungs.'

'Maybe, but it's very pleasurable,' Murdo said as he exhaled smoke in the divinity student's direction. He picked a shard of tobacco from his tongue. 'Tell me, why do you call an accordion the instrument of the devil?'

'Because people dance to it.'

'They do, and they love it,' the musician conceded. 'Have you never danced yourself?'

'They tried to make me dance at school but my mother put a stop to it.'

'So what do you do for pleasure, Donald, if you don't smoke and you don't dance? Do you take a dram?'

His roommate looked at him with horror.

'I read the Bible.'

'Fair enough. I'll leave you to it,' Murdo said, slinging his accordion over his shoulder and leaving the divinity student to Revelations.

He went downstairs to explore the Hall. Men were sitting talking in the public rooms. He noted that many of them were wearing new blazers with the university badge of bell, book and bird embroidered in gold thread on the pocket above the heart and had on their new undergraduate ties which they had bought after matriculating because it was the rule that collar and tie had to be worn in the public rooms.

'Ah, we have a musician among us!' one of them shouted, and called Murdo across. 'Give us a tune.'

Murdo sat down in the group of half a dozen and, having introduced himself and exchanged handshakes, slipped his hands under the straps and began to play a reel. The students beat out the rhythm on the arms of their chairs and tapped their leather-soled brogues on the boards. More men gathered round the impromptu ceilidh, some of them puffing on pipes which still had to be broken in. By the end of his set of reels and strathspeys Murdo had made many new friends and for the rest of his time in residence in Maclay Hall would be called upon to play for birthday parties and celebrations such as shinty victories over other universities.

Four rooms in the spacious elegant building were set aside for quiet study and already freshmen were reading their newly purchased textbooks, continuing the studiousness they had shown at school. There was a squash court for the energetic, a billiard room for the indolent, a music room and a library. In the attached garage the affluent kept their cars and motor cycles.

As he walked up the path to the Hall, Dr Murdo Maclean was looking forward to a tour of inspection of his old Glasgow home. But as he approached he could see the sky through the roof of the château-style building. He was so upset by the sight of the shell that he had to clutch at a railing.

'Are you all right?' a woman exercising her West Highland terrier on a running line asked him.

'What happened to the Hall?' Murdo asked weakly.

'It went on fire a few years ago.'

'How did it happen?' its former resident asked.

'No one knows for sure. Some say it was a workman's blowlamp.'

'Were there students in it at the time?' Dr Maclean wanted to know.

'Oh no. The university had sold it and it was being developed.'

'I was a student here.'

Her look as she reeled in the inquisitive terrier implied that it must have been a long time ago.

'I've lived here all my life and I used to watch the students going down through the park to classes,' she reminisced. 'They were a polite, well behaved lot – not like today's students. They drink and take drugs in the park and I've seen couples –' The sentence was left unfinished as the dog was brought to heel.

Murdo gazed up at the empty window where he had stood smoking, looking down to couples strolling hand in hand through the park in the twilight while, at his back, the divinity student read aloud from the Bible about the deadly temptations of the flesh.

'They say that work on the building has stopped because of the economic situation,' the woman informed him as she and the tartan-collared pedigree terrier went home to the complete terrace house she had inherited from her lawyer father.

Murdo went disconsolately down the slope to his hotel, and after a disturbed sleep in which the flame of a match lighting a resident's pipe in Maclay Hall became an inferno, he decided that he would try to quell his sad heart with a meal. He passed a curry house but decided that the menu was too fiery for his digestion. He went into a small restaurant and ordered a chicken dish because he got plenty of fresher fish at home.

An hour later he continued on his pilgrimage of the Glasgow he had known, going along Berkeley Street to the Highlanders' Institute where he had played in a band. He was sure he was at the correct address, but the building in front of him was a block of stylish flats. He went into the nearby Mitchell Library to enquire. The pleasant woman fetched several books and was able to tell him that the Highlanders' Institute in Berkeley Street, which had moved from Elmbank Street in the early 1960s, had closed in the

1970s.

'Have you any photographs of it?' Dr Maclean asked.

The librarian went to a filing cabinet and flicked through polythene envelopes.

'I'm afraid not.'

On the way back to his hotel Murdo decided to make a detour. He was looking for the Grand Hotel which had stood at Charing Cross and in which he had played several times for weddings. Was he in the wrong place? He was standing looking up at a tall concrete building where he thought the Grand had been, and when a man passed, he asked for help.

'That was before my time,' the stranger informed him and passed on.

Dr Maclean went back to his hotel, ordered a whisky and sat in the lounge. It had been a mistake, coming to Glasgow on a sentimental pilgrimage. The city had been ruthlessly developed, the landmarks and haunts of his student days gone.

'Do you know what happened to the Grand Hotel?' he asked the waitress.

'I'm afraid not, sir.'

'It was demolished to make way for a road,' a voice from across the lounge informed him.

He turned to see a woman about the same age as himself sitting reading a magazine. 'I'm Annie Lorimer. I used to live in Glasgow in the 1960s.'

'I was at university here,' the doctor informed her. 'I used to play in a dance band.'

'Where?'

'In the Highlanders' Institute, the St Andrew's Halls, the

Grand Hotel – and other places.'

'I was a waitress for a season in the Grand Hotel,' she told him. 'Which band did you play in?'

'Hector MacLeod's.'

'I loved that sound. It was so vigorous, so full of energy. I danced to it in the Highlanders' Institute.'

'I played second accordion,' Murdo informed her, so grateful that he had found someone who remembered the Glasgow of his student days. Perhaps he had noted this attractive woman in a Strip the Willow set on the floor, being whirled on the arms of the men.

'You're Canadian?' he queried.

'No, Scottish, but when I went out to Montreal when I was twenty five I acquired a Canadian burr – not intentionally, you understand. I just seemed to become absorbed in the community. I studied law here and did an additional degree so that I could practise in Canada. And you?'

He explained that he had just retired as a GP from his west coast practice.

'Where did you live when you were here?'

'I was in Maclay Hall.'

'I was in Queen Margaret Hall in Bute Gardens for three years and I loved it. I shared with a girl from Dunoon, a lovely person. I kept up with her until she died two years ago, and if I could have come over for her funeral, I would have. Have you kept up with your university friends? You can do so on Facebook, on the computer.'

He explained that he had become rather isolated in his west coast practice, though occasionally classmates would drop in from yachts. But he had no best friend from university days. 'I don't know what happened to the divinity student I shared with in Maclay Hall, but I wouldn't be surprised if he became a Moderator. The sad thing is, Maclay isn't a university hall any more. I was up there this afternoon. It's a burnt-out shell. '

'Queen Margaret Hall isn't in Bute Gardens any longer. I went looking for it yesterday. Everything changes, but at least we have the memories. I'm retiring next year and I came to Glasgow to see if I would like to settle back here. I'm like you – I've been wandering about old haunts.'

'Will you come back here to live?' Dr Maclean asked.

'I don't think so. Too many of my landmarks have gone.'

He thought seriously of inviting this attractive woman, who was staying in the hotel, to have lunch with him the following day so that they could exchange reminiscences of Glasgow over forty years before. Not that there was any chance of him starting an affair at his age, when he had counselled so many broken marriages in his practice.

'Every city changes,' the Canadian citizen philosophised. 'Montreal certainly has in the time I've been there, but Glasgow more than most. If I hadn't bought a map I wouldn't have been able to find my way around, yet there's nothing wrong with my memory. They demolished buildings here because they were in the way of roads. They never thought of their architectural merit.'

'The point about Glasgow was that it contained a community of people from the Highlands and Islands,' the retired physician explained to his elegant listener. 'There were a lot of people from the island I came from, at the university, working in shops and offices, sailing up the river in cargo ships. I played for them in the Highlanders' Institute and when I was training to be a doctor I attended to them in the Western Infirmary.' He smiled as he shook his head in fond memory. 'There was one woman in particular, Mary Ann Mackinnon, who welcomed the people from our island to Glasgow.'

2. Cream Horns

People coming from the island to Glasgow to work or on holiday were assured of a warm welcome in Doig the bakers, which was a few minutes walk down from Buchanan Street Railway Station and which also had a section for serving meals. When Mary Ann Mackinnon recognised them from behind the counter she would shout: 'Take a seat, I'll be with you in a minute!' When she had finished serving the customer she would come round, give the new arrival a hug and ask them what they wanted to eat. If they had come off a morning train she would say: 'I'm sorry we don't serve kippers, but I can give you two eggs, fried or as you wish, bacon, sausages, black pudding and tea or coffee.'

Or, if it were the late afternoon, high tea would be offered, with haddock and chips, scones, a pot of tea and also a cake. Since it was a long way from the island by boat and train, the new arrival would usually request a full meal and Mary Ann would head for the kitchen, bumping open the swing door with her backside. She was thirty two years of age and seventeen stones without her shoes, her bulk caused by helping herself from the counter. At a quiet time she would pick up a pastry and before stuffing it into her mouth, would say: 'Doig's won't miss this one, not with the money they're making in this shop.' For lunch she would have a pie or bridie on the house, perhaps followed by an apple turnover. There was nobody to check her, since she was the manageress. Doig was part of a chain and in her ten years in the bakery she had never met one of the Doig family. Once a week a thin-lipped woman, Miss Robson, an accountant evidently, came in with the pay packets and departed with the takings from the safe. There was never a stocktaking, because cakes disappeared off the glass shelves very quickly, into customers' bags, or Mary Ann's mouth.

This afternoon the islander who has come into the shop is called Seumas MacNiven. He's in his early twenties. As he was going up the gangway on to the steamer on the island the piermaster said to him: 'you'll need a good feed when you get to Glasgow, so go into Doig the bakers in Buchanan Street and ask for Mary Ann Mackinnon.'

Mary Ann knows who he is and comes round the counter to welcome him in a muscular embrace that leaves him breathless. Will he have tea or coffee with his high tea? He elects to have coffee, because he thinks that that's what sophisticated people drink in the city. There are two cases under the table, a cardboard one containing his clothes, and a wooden one containing his bagpipes. Seumas has come to the city to join the Glasgow police. In his application he mentioned he was a piper and he'd been instructed: 'bring your pipes to the interviews.'

Mary Ann brings his high tea and a napkin, the first he's ever used. She sits down beside him, interrogating him as he enjoys the fried fish. So he's going to join the Glasgow police? He hopes to, he corrects her, but he still has to pass a medical and a test. 'Och, you'll get through these no bother,' she says with a dismissive wave. 'A fine strapping lad like you will have no difficulty. Where are you going to stay?'

'In Ashley Street, with Mrs MacCaig. She emigrated to the city from the island forty years before and lets out rooms in her spacious flat to those coming down to the city from her home island to work or on holiday.' Mary Ann tells the newcomer that Phemie MacCaig is a relative of hers and that she'll come round to see him there one night soon, once he's settled in.

'How much?' he asks, after he has cleaned the plate with the piece of bread and consumed the iced biscuit with the cherry on top.

'It's on the house,' Mary Ann tells him grandiosely. It's been the same for every person from the island who's come into the bakery in the ten years that she's worked there. It must have cost Mr Doig (if he exists) hundreds of pounds, though, evidently, the manageress has no compunction about sharing the profits with her fellow islanders, as well as feeding herself from the shelves of the shop. She has been known to eat three cream horns in succession, and still have room for an Empire biscuit.

The prospective police cadet picked up his suitcase and

Maclay Days

pipes and is told by Mary Ann which bus to take to get to Ashley Street. 'Be sure you ask off at Woodlands Road.' Half an hour later Seumas is climbing to Mrs MacCaig's top floor apartment in Ashley Street, the steps worn concave by the feet of many islanders. Phemie MacCaig is a small woman who habitually dresses in black, though not out of mourning for her husband, who fell drunk into the Clyde and whose corpse came ashore at Bowling. She leads the new arrival into a room which, she explains, he has to share with someone else from the island.

Later that night Seumas, who was sitting practising his chanter playing, met his new bedfellow, Dougie McCormick. Seumas didn't know him, but they shook hands and exchanged greetings in Gaelic. Dougie was in his early forties and was wearing a black suit and tie, so Seumas asked if he had had a bereavement. Oh no, he was an undertaker with an old established city firm. Seumas didn't fancy sharing a bed with a man who dealt in death, but there was nowhere else to lay his head. He was wakened at midnight by a sound which suggested that there was a wild beast in the room, but it was Dougie snoring.

A week later Mary Ann appeared at the flat, with a box of doughnuts from Doig tied with blue ribbon, and a half bottle of whisky which she had purchased in Bells Bar on her way to Ashley Street.

'How did Seumas get on?' she asked when she was sitting by the coal-burning range in the kitchen where Mrs MacCaig held court.

'He'll tell you himself,' and she went through to summon him from his room.

'Well, are you a police cadet?' Mary Ann wants to know.

Seumas tells her the story. First of all he went for his medical. The doctor told him to remove all his clothes and then examined him. Seumas doesn't tell his two female listeners that he was asked to bend over. The doctor had tapped his chest with two fingers and listened to his heart through a stethoscope.

'You're in very good shape,' he told his patient. 'That's all the mackerel you eat on the islands.'

Seumas didn't tell him that he had an aversion to mackerel. Two days later he went for his interview. There were two policemen in the room, their hats on the table in front of them.

'There's a wee problem to you joining the Glasgow force,' one of them disclosed. 'You're half an inch short.'

'Never mind that,' the second man said dismissively. 'Let's hear your pipes.'

As Seumas played them a strathspey and reel they were tapping the ends of their pencils on the table. While he was folding his pipes into their box the second policeman was telling his colleague: 'I think the doctor must have misread this lad's height.'

'Then we'll need to get him re-measured, that's all there is to it.'

'What's half an inch here or there to a piper?' the second policeman asked.

'What do you mean?' his colleague wanted to know.

'No need to get him re-measured. He'll fit in fine with the police band.' He stood up and extended a hand: 'Congratulations, son, you're a member of the Glasgow police – and our pipe band. There's a practice on Friday night. I'll give you the address.'

Mary Ann poured a libation for her hostess, and an equally generous one for herself to toast Seumas's success. He refused a whisky, because he belonged to a rare phenomenon on the island, and among the piping fraternity – a family of teetotallers. But he ate a Doig doughnut as they reminisced about the island. Mrs MacCaig asked him to give them a tune on the pipes.

'Won't the neighbours complain?' Mary Ann asked.

'The man through the wall is from Skye. He's delighted that we've got a piper on the stairs.'

As he stood marking time in the kitchen Seumas gave the two women a selection of tunes inspired by the island's mountains and lochs, its mists and lovesick maidens. There were tears in Mrs MacCaig's eyes as she listened, not because she was remembering her drowned spouse, but because she was seeing again the croft she had come from on the island, where the hens roosted on the backs of the chairs and the floor was sprinkled with white sand she and her sisters had lugged up in a pail from the shore. There had been no electricity, no running water and their toilet had consisted of a board with a circular hole and bucket below in a rusted corrugated iron lean-to against the side of the house, strips of the local paper (including births and deaths notices) hanging on a rusty nail. As for Mary Ann, her memories, as she listened to the mellifluous medley, were of a small house at the top of the town, with only Gaelic spoken, net curtains on the window, and a wireless with an accumulator on the sill. But there were even more powerful emotions as she watched the fingers of the handsome young piper fluttering up and down the holes of the ebony chanter. As soon as he had walked into the bakers she had taken a fancy to him, though she knew that she was at least ten years his senior.

Though Mary Ann was well known among island exiles in the city, little was known about her domestic circumstances. There was talk that when she first came to Glasgow, and before her consumption of Doig's stock had doubled her weight, she had married a man from another island who was in the Merchant Navy. Nobody could recall any details about the wedding, but it was believed that her husband, absent for ten months of the year at sea, had got drunk one night in a Canadian port and had gone home with a woman of Indian blood. It could have been a tale concocted by a malicious crew member on the same ship, but nobody had ever seen this mysterious seafarer and there was no ring on Mary Ann's hand.

'That was beautiful!' she exclaimed, applauding when the piping recital was finished. 'When will you get your uniform?'

'You mean my police uniform, or pipe band uniform? I'll get measured for the band uniform on Friday night.'

'How will the band fit in with your duties as a policeman?' Mrs MacCaig enquired.

'They said that I'll be on day shift all the time and that I'll get time off in the week for band practice.'

Mary Ann was very interested in this information because on Sunday afternoons she would go to Bellahouston Park to listen to the police pipe band playing, a bag of Doig's cakes beside her and a straw hat with a Mackinnon tartan ribbon on her head. When they played at a concert she would get a free ticket in exchange for the cakes she handed out to pipe band members in the bakers. She loved pipe music and had several records which she played on the Dansette she had bought at the Barrows for a pound. The tenants next door to the second floor flat she rented in New City Road would pound on the wall when she played a pipe band record, and she would go and turn up the volume until it felt as if the whole tenement was vibrating. Once they sent for the police, but it so happened that the constable who attended the complaint was a Gael who sometimes dropped in off his beat for a cake and a cup in Doig's and instead of cautioning her he sat down to a sumptuous afternoon tea and a Gaelic conversation with her.

'You must come into the shop and tell me when you're playing in public,' she instructed Seumas.

The following week he appeared in Doig's in his police uniform.

'You look so smart!' Mary Ann exclaimed as she set down a cream puff and a cup of sweet tea in front of him. 'Have you made your first arrest yet?'

'Nothing like that,' he said wryly. 'I'm on car parking duty. A man left his car up on the pavement in front of the Highlanders' Institute and I had to go in and tell him to remove it. He was from Harris and he swore at me.'

'I hope you arrested him,' Doig's manageress said vehemently.

'I gave him five minutes to remove it or I would phone for assistance, I told him.'

'Quite right,' Mary Ann said. 'These people from Harris have no manners. There's one who comes in here and drinks his tea from the saucer. "You're not in a black house at Luskentyre now," I told him. So when are you playing in public?'

'On Sunday, in Bellahouston Park.'

'I'll be there.'

On the Saturday afternoon Mary Ann kept back a selection of cakes for her own consumption and took them home on the bus in a neatly tied box on her substantial knees. The following day she put the cakes into a basket, with a thermos flask and used the same mode of conveyance to take her out to Bellahouston Park. It was a warm day under a cloudless sky and Mary Ann, who was wearing her straw hat, spread out the tartan rug she had brought with her under her ample hips and sat on the grass as close as possible to the band. The big drummer was twirling the fluffy sticks and the pipers' brogues were keeping time. Mary Ann's eyes were fixed on Seumas and she thought, with his bonnet with its black ribbon, that he looked even more handsome. When the band finished she called him over and they shared the picnic she had brought with her, including a pie with potato topping for the piper.

Seumas was naive about women. He had had a girlfriend for a week at his school on the island, but hadn't succeeded in kissing her at the Christmas hop. Therefore it never entered his head that Mary Ann had designs on him and that the crumpet that followed the pie was symbolic of this. She even produced a paper napkin with Doig's name, and the shop's emblem, a doughnut, on it.

'What are you doing on Friday night?' Mary Ann asked her companion.

'Nothing.'

'Do you want to go to the pictures?'

'What's on?' he asked.

Here Mary Ann, who always planned things so meticulously, had made an error by not looking up the cinema lists.

'I don't know, but I'll find out, and come up to Phemie's on the Thursday night to tell you.'

But on the Thursday afternoon a small man wearing a bowler hat that seemed too big was standing at the counter. He was small and Mary Ann had to lean over to see him.

'Yes?' she asked peremptorily.

'What's that you're eating?' he asked.

'It's a cream horn, but we haven't any left.'

'No wonder, if you're stuffing your face.'

'You cheeky bugger. Get out of here!'

'Why should I leave my own shop?'

Mary Ann began to feel faint behind the counter, as if she had consumed an excessive amount of sugar in the confections.

'I'm Mr Samuel Doig and now I see why the takings are down since you took over as manageress. You're eating my profits.'

Mary Ann had always been resourceful.

'I beg your pardon,' she said indignantly. 'I put the money for that cream horn into the till and I pay for everything I eat. The reason you're takings are down, Mr Doig, is that we have stock left at the end of the day which I have to throw out. I heard of a case in Rutherglen of a cream puff being sold the following day and giving the customer food poisoning. She sued and was awarded a substantial sum. I'm trying to protect your reputation, Mr Doig, even if there is some wastage.'

'That's very thoughtful of you,' he conceded. 'I'm looking for a manageress for our shop in New City Road. It's a busy place, with half a dozen staff. Will you go there?'

Mary Ann shook her head. 'I know what the customers want and I prefer to stay here. But thank you for the offer, Mr Doig. It's good to meet you at last,' she added, and leaned over the counter to extend a firm hand to the wee man.

3. The Accordion
with the Curved Keyboard

Murdo Maclean wondered how the highly strung theological student, with whom he shared a room in Maclay Hall, would ever be able to deliver a comprehensible sermon with his stutter. Besides which, there seemed to be no tradition of taking baths in Sutherland and Murdo was forced to try to sleep with the window open on the city. It was still noisy though the trams had gone.

Some of the occupants of the Hall seemed to have come to university with the intention of consuming as much whisky and doing as little work as possible. Iain MacGilp had black hair which was slicked back and very fine features, particularly around the expressive eyes. He favoured hounds-tooth jackets and tailored black trousers. He had matriculated to study philosophy but seldom went to classes. If he weren't found in the snooker room, chalking a cue, he would be in the Halt Bar down on Woodlands Road. He had a remarkable capacity for whisky and seemed to become even more urbane. In the evenings he put on patent leather shoes with pointed toes and went dancing in the Locarno or in the Highlanders' Institute, because he was equally accomplished in jiving and ceilidh dancing and never lacked partners. In fact a girl from Barra broke an ankle running across the floor to secure him in a Ladies' Choice in the Highlanders one Friday evening. He bought her a fruit squash and sat massaging her foot until she was taken away to have it in encased in plaster for six weeks, during which period she put on weight which she never shifted.

Murdo Maclean knew that he had demanding years in medicine in front of him and that if he fell behind in his studies, he would be thrown out of the university. So every morning, with his new university scarf wrapped round his neck, he walked with fellow students through the autumnal appeal of Kelvingrove Park to the medical building and sat through lectures on chemistry, physics and biology, as well as attending laboratory classes in these same subjects. A man called Neil Brogan, who had a crewcut and a reconstituted ear that had almost been ripped off in a rugby scrum, fulminated: 'We did all this science at Fettes. I want to do real medicine.'

'What do you mean by real medicine?' Murdo asked mildly.

The conversation was taking place in the Men's Union, with a cluster of pint glasses on the table.

'I mean, bodies, man, bodies.'

Maclay Days

'But we don't do anatomy until the second year,' Charlie Telfer pointed out as he deftly rolled himself a cigarette, as if he had spent his youth watching cowboy films. 'That's when you'll get to work on your first stiff. But you may be in for a big fright.'

'Are you implying that I'm going to faint at the sight of a corpse?' Brogan challenged him.

'No, but a girl I know who's in third year medicine says that when she opened a vat for the first time her granny was lying in it. Evidently she had bequeathed her body to medical science.'

'That is one of the oldest stories in medicine – as old as Lister!' Brogan shouted.

On the evening of this exchange Murdo had a visitor at the Hall. The small stocky man identified himself as Hector MacLeod.

'I've heard your band on the wireless,' Murdo said with admiration.

'Alasdair MacTavish phoned me to say that you were coming to Glasgow to study and that I was to sign you up before anyone else did because you're a bloody good accordionist. I need a second box player for Friday night down the road at St Andrew's Halls. It's the usual stuff, Gay Gordons, waltzs, eightsome reels.'

'I don't have music for the eightsome,' Murdo told him.

'We don't use written-down music. It's all in here,' Hector said, tapping his temple. 'You'll soon pick up the tunes. Anyway, you'll be playing chords.'

Murdo didn't consult his parents about his debut in the Glasgow musical scene because he knew they would say he was wasting time he should be using to study and besides, MacLeod's band were known to be hard-drinking.

'I'll be pleased to play.'

Assuming that he had hired a new member of the band, Hector took him round to West-End Misfits in Queen's Arcade and kitted him out with an evening suit that had shiny lapels and stripes running down the legs of the trousers. It had been made for an older client who had died before he could take delivery, but Hector pointed out to his new band member that he could hitch up the trousers. On the Friday evening, wearing his new suit, Murdo carried his accordion case slung on his shoulder down into the Grand Hall in St Andrew's Halls at Charing Cross. He had never been in such a massive hall before and was awed by the splendour of the organ. There must have been five hundred dancers on the floor at the Highland Ball, with plenty of room to spare. After the first few nervous tunes, Murdo began to settle into the band. Behind him Charlie plucked the strings of the double bass, and at the piano Gordon was a ramping virtuoso. Wee Neilly was on drums, making the cymbal shimmer when he struck it and on the lead accordion, Hector fingered out the Gaelic waltz as the dancers swept round the floor in perfect form-ation, the women in long gowns, with gloves up to their elbows, the men in Highland evening dress, square silver buttons on their doublets and cairngorm-hilted *sghian dubhs* down their hose.

As he fingered the keyboard Murdo was watching a dark-haired beauty hopping round the floor in the Canadian Barn Dance. When they came close to the platform she smiled up at him and this encouraged Murdo to play with even more eloquence so that Hector nodded and smiled in approval to him. At the interval Murdo searched for the dark-haired dancer. He saw her standing with a group of other young women so he lingered nearby.

'You're new in the band?' she said as she came up to him.

'This is my first night.'

'You fit in very well. I could hear your chords as I passed. My name's Una MacTaggart and I'm from Islay.'

Murdo explained that he too was a Hebridean, from an island nearer the mainland.

'And are you a full-time musician?' Miss MacTaggart enquired.

'I'm a medical student.'

'You must be brainy.'

He shook his head. 'And you?'

'I'm much lower down the medical scale. I'm a nurse in the Western Infirmary. I did try for medical school, but I wasn't bright enough.'

The band was going back on to the platform for the second half, so Murdo had to think fast.

'Can I see you home?'

'How do you know I don't have a boyfriend?'

'I'm assuming.'

'Don't assume anything about women from Islay. They're dangerous,' she breathed in his ear.

'Am I seeing you home?'

'Possibly – depending on how well you play in the second half.'

Una was taken up for nearly every dance and Murdo wished he were down on the floor, spinning her in Strip the

Willow, or with her cheek against his in the Gaelic waltz. The band played *Auld Lang Syne* as the dancers made a huge circle round the hall. Murdo was searching for his date, but couldn't see her anywhere and wondered if she had slipped away. Probably she had been teasing him. The evening that had been so euphoric was ending in depression. He put his accordion back into its case, covering the keyboard with the velvet cloth, and lugged it off the stage.

'Are you coming for a drink?' Hector Macleod asked.

But he declined the invitation because he suspected that it would be an all-night session. Una was waiting for him at the door, in a blue cape with a hood.

'I thought you were going to stand me up,' she rebuked him.

'I thought you'd gone.'

'This isn't a threesome,' she told him.

'What do you mean?' the shy young medical student asked.

'You're not lugging that accordion about with you.'

'I'll leave it with the janitor.'

When he came back he took her arm and they walked up Woodlands Road, through to Byres Road. Some evenings, when the food in the hall wasn't to his liking, Murdo came down from the heights of Maclay Hall on to Byres Road for a fish supper at Bambino Salveta's. Murdo thought that the name sounded like that of an opera singer who had performed at La Scala and certainly the man behind the counter sang in his native language as he trawled the fried haddock from the bubbling fat.

'Do you fancy a fish supper?' Murdo asked his date.

It seemed to be a love song that the Latin was crooning

as he shook salt and pepper over the golden crust, wrapped it in brown paper and then in newspaper.

'What do you think of that?' Una asked, stopping at a window where there was a dummy of a Teddy boy in a long jacket with a velvet collar and tight drainpipe trousers.

Murdo waited until he had chewed the thick acrid chip before answering.

'It looks scary.'

'I quite like it,' she mused. 'I think it would suit you.' She ruffled his hair. 'However, you would have to do something about that.'

'What's wrong with it?' he asked.

'It looks as if it's been cut with sheep shears. You need a more trendy cut. How about a duck's arse?'

'What's that?' he asked, shocked.

'It's what Teddy boys wear.' She lifted her hands to his head and brushed the hair at the back into two wings. 'Like that. Then all you would need is a pair of suede shoes with thick soles and I'd be walking out with a Teddy boy.'

'Are there Teddy boys on Islay?' he asked.

'Come on Murdo. Most of the men wear dungarees and caps back to front. All they talk about is shearing sheep and the price of fuel for their tractors.'

He was enchanted by the banter and vitality of this pretty young woman eating her fish supper so elegantly, then carefully compressing the greasy paper into a ball and depositing it in a wire bin affixed to a lamp post.

'Where do you live?' he asked.

'I'm in the nurses' quarters at the Western Infirmary. But I don't want to go in yet. Will you take me for a coffee?'

'Where would you like to go?'

'The Silver Slipper in Great Western Road.'

The café beside the Botanic Gardens was open late with young people who had come to the studio in the building to take dance lessons. Some of them were lonely and wanted to learn to dance so that they could meet someone in one of the city's many ballrooms. They were wearing lounge suits and dresses, and several of them, who had only met that evening as they helped each other in the intricacies of the foxtrot, were already holding hands.

Murdo watched Una cradling the transparent cup of coffee between her hands, licking off the froth. He knew that he was smitten. Outside the nurses' quarters he was permitted a brief kiss before she hurried inside, after agreeing to meet him on the following Saturday afternoon in the University Café. That week Murdo found his mind wandering in his medical classes as he thought about the young woman in the blue cloak who had taken his arm and who had allowed him to lift down the hood and kiss her. He made a basic mistake in the chemistry of the body and was rebuked by his tutor.

Murdo was forced to be an early riser in Maclay Hall because his roommate, the divinity student Donald Gunn, rose at seven, and having done his noisy exercises, including fifty press-ups, read aloud from the Bible. On this late October morning Murdo went to the window and opened the curtains to check the weather.

'What's that glow in the sky?' he enquired.

His roommate came to the window.

'The ci-city of Babel is on fi-fire.'

'What the hell does that mean?' Murdo asked truculently.

'There's no need to swear,' he was rebuked.

'It's a big fire,' Murdo observed.

He went to wash and shave and at eight descended the stairs to breakfast. As he was passing into the dining-room he heard two of the female staff talking.

'I saw it when I came up,' one was saying. 'It's St Andrew's Halls.'

'What about St Andrew's Halls?' Murdo butted in.

'They're on fire.'

As Murdo made for the front door he almost knocked down one of the maids. He ran along Park Terrace and down the steps, the driver of a milk float yelling at him to watch where he was going as he sprinted across Sauchiehall Street. The whole sky seemed to be lit up as he approached the Halls. Fanned by a strong breeze, flames were roaring through the building. Murdo saw half a dozen firemen perched on eighty feet high turntable ladders, directing thousands of gallons of water into the inferno.

'My accordion's in there!' Murdo shouted, trying to push forward. He had left it with a porter after the dance the previous Friday and had decided to leave it for the following Friday's dance at the Highlanders' Institute.

'You're not going in there, son,' a policeman cautioned him.

The paintwork of cars in the street was bubbling and there was the burnt-out skeleton of a motor cycle ignited by a spark. Residents had gathered from adjacent streets, some of the women with their hair in curlers. Murdo watched optimistically as a basket containing sheet music was brought out undamaged from the basement of the Halls, followed by instruments belonging to the Scottish National Orchestra who were due to play in the Halls that evening. He waited to see the black case containing his accordion emerging, but there was no sign of it. The ivory keys would have melted in the inferno.

Murdo went back up to Maclay Hall, disconsolate. When he told the theological student that it was St Andrew's Halls and not the Mitchell Library that was being consumed by fire, Donald Gunn smiled.

'Vi-Vengeance is mine, saith the Lord.'

'What do you mean by that?' Murdo asked angrily.

'It was a di-den of iniquity, with all that da-dancing,'

That afternoon when he met Una in the University Café on Byres Road he told her about the catastrophe.

'You can get an accordion at the Barrows,' she suggested.

'The Barrows?'

'You've never heard of the Barrows? We'll go there tomorrow afternoon.'

They went down to Argyle Street by bus and walked along to the market. Murdo was awed by the dozens of stalls with vendors holding up goods and extolling the unrepeatable value to the crowd.

'Two sheets, two blankets – a great bargain at three pounds, and ah'll throw in the pillowcases free,' the vendor promised the mesmerised crowd. 'How about you, lassie?' he shouted to Una. 'Are ye no' thinkin' o' settin' up a home wi' yer friend there? The way he's holdin' yer arm, he seems feared that someone will steal ye.'

Una asked directions and led Murdo to a stall where accordions were set out. There was one with a curved keyboard which took his fancy and he asked the stallholder if he could try it.

'That's a classic instrument, a Cooperativa L'Armonica Stadella Super de Luxe,' the vendor informed him.

Murdo loved the name as much as the tune he was playing on the mother-of-pearl instrument.

'How much?'

'Forty pounds, son.'

'I can't afford that,' Murdo said sadly as he unstrapped the instrument that seemed to have been made for his body.

'The price isn't correct,' Una told the man. 'It's thirty five pounds.'

'I said forty.'

'And I said thirty five because I'm paying. '

'I can't allow you to buy this for me,' Murdo told her.

'It isn't a present. I expect to be paid back at the rate of five pounds per month.'

'That will take seven months,' Murdo pointed out.

'Why, don't you expect our relationship to last that time? And there's a further catch, Murdo. Islay people are always looking for that wee bit extra, so a fortnight Friday you'll be playing for us at the nurses' annual dance.'

As Una was writing a cheque, Murdo played a reel. A couple standing nearby began to dance and in no time at all there was a set for Strip the Willow.

On the date, he turned up at the hall where the nurses' annual dance was taking place, his new accordion slung on his back. He had already been playing it in the band and to a group of fellow residents in Maclay and he loved the curving keyboard and the mellow tone, as if the previous owner had been a gifted musician and had invested it with his love and his skills. It seemed to play itself between his hands as he fingered out a Gaelic waltz – until he saw Una dancing with a man and then the tune changed abruptly. At the interval for food Murdo asked who his rival was.

'A doctor I work with. You're not jealous, are you?'

'Not a bit.'

But he saw that it was the wrong answer and in the waltz he played in the second half, her partner held her close, and when she passed Murdo she looked at him dreamily.

4. Rejection

Donald Gunn came from the north of Scotland, from a county whose population had been cleared extensively to make way for more profitable flocks of sheep in the nineteenth century. The people had huddled on the shore, surviving on shellfish and faith before being shipped across to Canada where many of them had perished before they could establish homesteads with the axe and plough. In one church, Donald's forebears had listened fearfully to the minister condemning their wickedness in opposing the laird by refusing to go on the emigrant ship which he had hired 'at great cost to himself,' the minister fulminated. He was so worked up that he seemed in danger of falling from the high pulpit. After the fiery sermon, the congregation had used a nail from one of the demolished homesteads to scratch on a pane of the church: 'we are the wicked generation.'

Donald's people had evaded transportation by hiding in the hills and in time emerged to build homesteads in a glen that couldn't sustain sheep. It was a backbreaking existence, digging lazy beds among the rocks then trying to grow potatoes and grain in the thin windswept soil. The admission that they had etched on the window of the church never left them and they believed that however hard they prayed and however exemplary a life they led, they were doomed. If there were any chance of forgetting this judgement, it was reinforced by itinerant preachers who walked into the glen, in high black hats and with collars cutting into their throats. Donald's father was a crofter who had been denied further education because he didn't have the wherewithal for the shoes and the barrel of salted herring to take him to Glasgow. When his son went, he was assisted by a bursary arranged by the laird, through a Society desperately dedicated to the preservation of Gaelic. It was a condition of this subsistence that the recipient study Celtic. A native Gaelic speaker, Donald wanted to strengthen his command of the language so that he could deliver terrifyingly eloquent sermons when he qualified as a minister, though he knew that his stutter worsened when he became worked up.

Donald was successful in gaining a place in Maclay Hall in Glasgow and found himself sharing with Murdo Maclean, an islander who was studying medicine, but who, unfortunately, didn't speak Gaelic. Every morning, irrespective of whether or not his roommate was awake, Donald read for twenty minutes from the Gaelic Bible and in the evening at nine o' clock he knelt by his bed in his pyjamas and said his prayers in the same sonorous language. This irritated Murdo, having grown up with a father who was fanatical about Gaelic, and who, though not overtly religious, kept a Gaelic Bible on the floor by his bedside for the pleasure of the beauty of the prose when he couldn't sleep, the anglepoise lamp's yellow circle on the gilt-edged page. While he read about the creation of the world, Archie Maclean ate sweets and when he crunched a hard centre, awoke his wife, who had no interest in learning Gaelic and who wanted her children to be citizens of an English-speaking world and whose own ambition was to live on the mainland again.

One evening in early Novembe, Murdo came in from a lecture to find Donald sitting sobbing in his room.

'Have you had bad news?' he enquired gently.

'Professor Mi-Matheson's dead.'

'Who's Professor Matheson?'

Donald looked at him indignantly. 'Professor Angus Mi-Matheson was the Professor of Celtic, one of the foremost sc-scholars of his generation, and the reason why I ch-chose to come to Glasgow University. I could have gone to Edinburgh or Ab-Aberdeen.'

'They'll replace him,' Murdo pointed out.

'They'll ne-never replace a man like that.'

Donald Gunn was never seen in the downstairs public rooms of Maclay Hall because he disapproved of all the activities that took place there. He wouldn't sit in the common room because of the smokers with their Capstan Full Strength cigarettes and their foul pipes. He wouldn't go within earshot of the radiogram, on which the latest posthumous releases by Buddy Holly and the already immortal Elvis were played incessantly. He would never set foot in the billiard room and he had no reason to enter the garage, because he didn't keep a vehicle of any kind.

When he heard a dirty joke at the supper table he would leave, even though he was only at the first course. He abided by every one of the Hall rules and only took one pat of butter and his fair share of milk for his porridge.

One evening Neil Brogan and Murdo Maclean were discussing the Celtic student over smokes.

'He's a queer bugger,' the rugby player observed, his feet up on the coffee table, since the warden wasn't on patrol. 'I bet you hear his bed springs going during the night.'

'It's not his hand that causes the noise, but his nostrils,' the medical student complained. 'I've never heard such snoring. I go across to his bed and dunt him, but as soon as I'm back in my own pit he starts up again.'

'If that was me being disturbed I would smother him with his pillow,' Brogan insisted. 'It would be a kindness to put him out of his misery. He's going to die a virgin – a blind one because he's always reading that Gaelic Bible. Can't you fix him up with a date?'

'He wouldn't keep it,' Murdo assured his friend.

'Why don't you ask for a shift of room?'

'Because it would offend him and because the warden wouldn't allow it. He told me that Mr Gunn needed bringing out of himself.'

'You're a much more patient man than I am, Murdo. Well, I must go,' he announced, swinging his legs from the table. 'I've arranged to meet a very nice little piece in the Rubaiyat Bar at eight.'

A week later a new waitress arrived in Maclay Hall. She was tall and attractive and had gold hoops dangling from her ears. She was swift and efficient at breakfast in the dining-room, and when she came to Donald Gunn's table she put an extra roll in front of him, though the strict rule was only one roll per resident – plus one pat of butter. But the waitress, who was called Teresa, brought a dish with an extra pat for Donald. He was both embarrassed and terrified, because he didn't know why he had been singled out for these acts of generosity by the new waitress and because if the warden came to hear that he was receiving extra rations, he would be rebuked. But rather than make a fuss in front of the other men, Donald ate the roll with the extra butter. As he did so the waitress winked at him and went through to the kitchen, hips swinging in her tight black skirt.

Donald was troubled that morning in the Celtic lecture, and failed to write down important information on grammar because he was thinking about the new waitress. He usually fasted at lunch time, but today he hurries back to the Hall for lunch in the hope that Teresa is still on duty. She is and smiles at him as she serves the students. The divinity student is feeling distinctly odd, not because he has eaten something that hasn't agreed with him, but because of the effect the new waitress's manner is having on his composure. He goes back to the university in the afternoon for classes, but when he returns to the Hall through the winter darkness, Teresa has gone. He finds himself pining for her as he eats his supper and when he goes up to the room he shares with Murdo Maclean, he can't concentrate on his Gaelic text. He stands at the window, looking out on the lighted city and wonders where Teresa lives and what she is doing that evening. Is she thinking about him? Will she be in for breakfast in the morning and will she continue to give him more than his due?

When Murdo comes up from practising a new pipe tune on his accordion in the music room, he finds that his roommate isn't reading the Gaelic Bible, the first night it hasn't been out on his bed.

'Is there something the matter?' he asks, concerned.

'Di-Did you notice anything at breakfast this morning?' Donald asks.

'What do you mean?'

'The new wi-waitress.'

'I noticed her all right. She's got very elegant legs. Don't tell me you've fallen for her.'

'She gave me an extra ri-roll and an extra pi-pat of butter.'

'I get it – you're frightened that the warden will order you to be flogged for taking extra rations. Don't be so stupid, Donald – take all you can get. If the new waitress smuggles you an extra fried egg, gobble it up.'

The next morning Teresa was in the dining-room and when Donald had cleaned his porridge plate she whispered in his ear: 'would you like some more?'

'It i-isn't allowed,' he told her hoarsely, terrified of her close proximity. As she leaned over to lift his plate, he closed his eyes to the temptation.

'Anything's allowed,' she told him and when she returned she had another steaming plate of porridge.

The rule was that the residents were only to take their 'fair share' of the milk, but Teresa tipped almost the entire contents of the jug on to the Celtic student's porridge plate.

He was conscious that the other men at the table were noting the special attention he was receiving and as he lifted the brimming spoon to his lips, he was in terror that the warden would come into the dining-room and accuse him of a violation of the rules of frugality.

'You're a lucky bastard, getting the attention of that one,' Neil Brogan nudged him.

The student who would be a minister of the Free Church shuddered at the profanity. But he seemed to be becoming a different person as he walked through the winter park to the university and he took in almost nothing of the lecture.

That evening he left his Bible on his bedside cabinet and went downstairs to the front lounge where a group of students were standing round the radiogram listening to a record that one of them had bought that afternoon. This was *Send Me the Pillow You Dream On* and as the Celtic student stood listening, he thought of Teresa's dark head lying on a pillow somewhere in the city which he knew so little about, apart from the location of the university and the church. As he listened to the song he began to realise that he was missing out on a great deal because of the strictly disciplined life of his upbringing.

The following morning, when Teresa brought him extra food, he asked her if she would like to go out with him. His invitation was delivered in a hesitant voice which he tried to keep to a whisper because of his stutter and of the alert ears on either side of him.

'We could go for a cup of tea.'

'That would be very nice,' she whispered to him as her presence came close in retrieving his plate. 'Where will we go?'

The suitor realised that he knew of no tea rooms in Glasgow.

'Where wi-would you like to go?' he asked.

'I've always fancied afternoon tea in the Grand Hotel.'

'Where's that?'

'You don't know where the Grand is? It's at Charing Cross. You can't miss it.'

'What time would you like to mi-meet?'

'I'm free at three o' clock this afternoon,' she informed him. 'We could meet at the entrance.'

Donald agreed to the rendezvous, but on the way up to the university, he remembered that he had a class at that hour. Should he go back and tell his date that they would have to fix another time? But suddenly, standing there on the path through the Park, its trees stripped bare, he became reckless for the first time in his life. He would miss the three o' clock class and keep his date.

Donald remained in Maclay after lunch, until the time of his rendezvous. Should he put on his dark Sunday suit for the first date of his life, or would his blazer, with its badge on the pocket, be more casual? He decided to keep on his blazer, but carefully combed his hair in the mirror and prayed that if he became excited, his stutter wouldn't let him down. He was at the entrance to the Grand Hotel half an hour before the appointed time. When Teresa appeared she was wearing an imitation fur coat and a very short kilt.

'I once applied for a job in here as a waitress, but I wasn't classy enough,' she told him as she thrust her arm through his and led him into the lounge of the hotel. Donald seemed to sink down into the sofa and she sat beside him, her thigh against his. When the waiter came up and asked what they wished, Donald replied: 'A pi-pot of tea for two, please.'

'Oh no,' his companion told the waiter. 'We'll have full afternoon tea for two.'

Donald watched in wonder and alarm as a tray of china was brought to the table, followed by three tiers of plates containing sandwiches and cakes. He watched as Teresa spread a napkin on her comely knees, cutting the sandwich with the dainty little silver knife provided.

'Pour the tea, Donald, please.'

His hand was shaking as he took up the silver pot, not only because he was nervous, but at the effect produced on him by the husky way she spoke his name. Some of the China infusion went over the table.

'Tell me about yourself,' she invited him as she munched a fruit slice.

He explained that he was from the north of Scotland and that he hoped to become a minister.

'Each to his own. I'm a Catholic myself.'

He heard the word with horror, recalling how much his parents despised the Church of Rome, insisting that the Free Church was the only true one in the sight of God. But his prejudices were overcome by the way in which she fished the fragment of fruit cake from her bosom and pushed it into her mouth with a scarlet-painted nail.

'You're a very attractive man.'

The tea he had just drunk seemed to have set fire to his insides and when she leaned over to kiss him on the mouth before taking another cake from the stand he thought he was going to faint. He felt even weaker when the waiter brought the bill and he practically had to empty his wallet on the table, beside the tier of plates which Teresa had cleared systematically.

'I'll take this as a souvenir,' she said, dropping the silver knife into her handbag.

He wanted to caution her that that was stealing, but he knew that he was in love with her.

'Wi-Where do you live?' he asked, when they were out on the pavement in the chilly twilight.

'In the east end,' she said vaguely. 'I'll get a bus a few streets up.'

'I'll wa-walk you there,' he volunteered.

'No need. See you in the morning.'

As he watched her walking up the street he wished fervently that he was going with her to a house where this time he would make the move as regards a kiss. But she was gone and he made his way disconsolately back to Maclay Hall, knowing with the amount he had spent on afternoon tea, that he would have to cut back for a week or so.

The following morning she was on duty in the dining-room.

'How do you fancy going to the pictures?' she asked.

'When?'

'Tonight.'

It was a romantic film, and the constant kissing in it made Donald bold. He put his arm round the shoulders of his date and drew her to himself as the suitor was doing on the screen. She lifted his hand and placed it on her knee. His heart was beating furiously underneath the gilded badge of his blazer, but he was too frightened to move.

Murdo Maclean was finishing breakfast when one of his friends came hurrying into the dining-room.

'You're needed,' he told the medical student.

'Why?'

'It's your roommate. He's gone off his head.'

The two students ran along Park Terrace to the imposing square tower of Trinity College. Donald Gunn had climbed up the internal steps and was standing on the balcony.

A crowd of male students from MacBrayne Hall and Kelvin Lodge as well as Maclay had gathered at the foot of the tower.

'How long has he been up there?' Murdo asked one of them.

'For about ten minutes.'

Suddenly the man above them shouted plaintively: 'I li-love her!'

'Who?' a student shouted back through cupped hands.

'Teresa.'

'Who's Teresa?' the man standing beside Murdo asked.

'She's one of the waitresses in our Hall. Evidently he's been going out with her.'

'I can't li-li- live without her!' the voice from above asserted.

The warden came striding along the Terrace.

'Come down at once, Gunn! You're disgracing the Hall!'

'But he isn't breaking a rule of Maclay Hall by throwing himself off a tower!' a voice called from the crowd.

'Perhaps he took an extra pat of butter!' someone else shouted.

The distraught Celtic student above was leaning over the

railing and sobbing: 'I bo-bought her afternoon tea in the Gr-Grand Hotel!'

'You're his roommate, Mr Maclean,' the warden addressed Murdo. 'It's better if you go up and fetch him down.'

As Murdo ascended the dark staircase he expected to hear a scream as the Celtic scholar propelled himself from the balcony in his delirium.

'Let's go and see Teresa, Donald,' he said gently as he stepped out behind him.

'Is she there?' he wailed.

'She's waiting for you in the Hall,' Murdo lied.

That evening, as Donald Gunn slept under sedation, Murdo had a conversation with Neil Brogan.

'How did he get entangled with the waitress in the first place?' Murdo wanted to know.

'I thought I was doing him a favour,' the rugby prop revealed. 'I told Teresa that he was the son of rich parents from the north and that he thought she was beautiful, so she made a play for him.'

'That was an insensitive thing to do,' Murdo rebuked him.

'Well, I thought she would have initiated him into the delights of the flesh before she discovered that he was a crofter's son with no money,' Brogan said with no show of guilt.

'You'll be next on her list,' Murdo warned.

'She's not my type,' the rugby playing medical student informed his friend. 'Too big in the skeletal structure.'

5. Deep Sea

When John Henderson was seventeen he left the island to go to the Royal Technical College in Glasgow, to its school of navigation. This was in the 1930s and there were unemployed men in caps and mufflers lounging at street corners with crossed ankles, waiting to act as bookies' runners, delivering betting slips for a sixpence. John lodged with a cousin in Shamrock Street and was assiduous in attending classes at the College. This was long before the age of computers and satellite navigation. He learned how to operate the electric signalling lamp and the gyroscope compass. He was taken up on to the roof observatory of the College for practical training in determining positions by the use of the sextant. He studied artificial horizons and also the stars through a reflector telescope mounted on a revolving platform.

At the weekend he went to the pub with the other

students. When he was a boy an uncle whose ship had unloaded at Hamburg brought him a mouth organ. John loved the gleaming instrument in the blue box and taught himself to play it. He lived on the croft with his widowed mother and some evenings she would ask him to fetch his harmonica and play her Gaelic tunes. He played the mouth organ in the Glasgow pub and customers came up and put a drink in front of him for the memories of their island homes that he had evoked, but he was careful how much he consumed.

On Saturday afternoons he went down to the Broomielaw, to watch cargo boats being loaded with provisions for the islands and to converse with the stevedores in Gaelic. Some evenings, sitting in his lodgings with a nautical textbook in front of him, his homesickness was almost unbearable, and he seriously considered giving up his navigation course and going home to work the croft. But he knew that his mother, who had high hopes for him, would be disappointed. She had had an uncle who had been on a windjammer going round the Cape in a ferocious storm and a brother who had been on Beatty's flagship at Jutland.

'The sea's running in your blood,' she reminded her son in Gaelic, the only language they used.

When he graduated he signed up with the Merchant Navy and within a year was using a sextant on the bridge of a vessel in the Indian Ocean. He loved his life at sea, the dolphins he saw, the ports they put into to discharge and load cargoes. When he went ashore he always took his mouth organ in his pocket and had been known to play Gaelic airs in a brothel in Zanzibar where a dusky woman danced, wearing nothing but a loop of beads. He was a moderate drinker – usually the wine of the country – and never needed assistance to get back on board ship. One night when they were at Halifax, Nova Scotia, loading timber, he woke to see his mother sitting smiling at him in the corner of his cabin and he knew that she had died. The telegram of confirmation came two days later, with the query by the neighbour who had sent it. *Will we hold funeral till you get back?* He wired back: *Go ahead with burial. Tell undertaker I'll settle account on my return in a month.*

When war broke out in 1939 he was transferred to minesweeping duties in the Western Approaches because of his knowledge of the waters. It was a dangerous patrol and at any time the vessel could be blown up by a U-boat or a mine. On VE Day, an airman returning from his last mission of the war saw the crew of the minesweeper dancing reels on the deck to a piper at the bow.

John Henderson didn't return to the Merchant Navy in peacetime. Instead he became mate on one of the Hebridean ferries and after five years was made Captain of the vessel that plied between the mainland and his native island. He wished his mother had been alive to see him bringing the ferry into the island port, standing on the bridge in his uniform, with gold braid on his sleeves and an anchor on his white-topped hat. One summer morning when the ferry was proceeding down the peaceful Sound he noticed a young woman standing at the railing. He picked up the binoculars and studied her face, then instructed the mate to take over the wheel while he went down on to the deck and approached the attractive passenger.

'If I'm not mistaken, it's Ishbel MacLeod,' he spoke to her in Gaelic.

'It is indeed,' she said, turning to greet him. 'And you're Captain John Henderson,' she added, touching his braided sleeve. 'You've come a long way from the wee lad who sat beside me in the primary class.'

'I have come a long way,' he conceded. 'I've been round the world several times with the Merchant Navy and God knows how many nautical miles the minesweeper I was on covered during the war. What are you doing with yourself?'

'I'm working on the reception desk of the Hebridean Hotel,' she told him, referring to the commodious establishment on the hill above the harbour in their native port.

'And are you liking it?'

'I like it fine. We're very busy in the summer. The same people come back, year in, year out, to the same rooms overlooking the bay. You get to know which newspapers they take and if they like a dram before bed. They leave good tips when they go and send me cards at Christmas.'

'It sounds to me as if you'll be marrying one of them yet,' the Captain said.

'I don't think so, John. I like my freedom too much.'

A week later, after the ferry was tied up for the night at the pier, he ascended the brae to the Hebridean Hotel. Ishbel was on duty at the reception desk and he stopped to speak to her.

'What are you doing up here?' she asked.

'I came up for a drink.'

'They must be paying you too much as a Captain.'

'I like to treat myself from time to time.'

He sat on a stool so that he could watch the reception desk through the glass door. When he saw her coming out with her coat on he put down his unfinished ale and followed her through the swing door.

'Can I walk you home?' he asked.

'It isn't very far.'

'Then we can make it further by taking a walk round the top of the town,' he suggested.

Though it was ten o' clock, it was summer and still light, so they sat on a bench, looking down over the bay.

'Don't you think this is the most beautiful place in the world?' she enthused.

'Many a night when I was on the merchant ship I wished that I was putting into the harbour here instead of one in South America,' he confessed.

'But you must have had a good time in these exotic places.'

He looked at this attractive woman. Was she suggesting that he had spent his shore leaves in bars and brothels, like some of the island men who had also served in the Merchant Fleet and who boasted of their conquests when they came home for good?

'I lived a very quiet life,' he informed her as he watched a brown-sailed skiff coming in after an evening's sail in the Sound. 'I'm pleased to be home – and in such good company.'

Every night he waited in the bar with a modest beer and walked her home, shining the big torch at her feet, his arm wrapped protectively around her against the autumn breeze. Six months later they were married in the Church of Scotland on a blustery day which threatened to carry the bride's veil out across the bay. John had kept his parents' croft house on the outskirts of the town and he modernised it, bringing in running water, electricity and a flushing toilet.

Within the year Ishbel was pregnant. She had given up her post in the Hebridean Hotel and ran the house efficiently. His supper was always waiting for him when the ferry tied up at six. She gave him nutritious meals, making pots of soup from the vegetables she grew, sprinkling the snowy potatoes with parsley she cut with scissors. When the child was born he helped her to bathe the boy before putting him to bed. On light nights he would go out to dig the croft and tend the dozen sheep that he kept. He sang in the Gaelic choir and would have a single dram with the members in the Arms before climbing the brae. At New Year the house was always full of people and he would play Gaelic requests on his mouth organ but would be up early the following morning to take the ferry down the Sound to the mainland. He was spoken of as the next Commodore of the steamer fleet.

A year after the boy, Ruari, there was a girl, Sileas. On Sundays he would push the pram down the brae to the church, where he was an elder, handing out the hymn books in the blue-carpeted vestibule while Mrs Mackenzie tramped out solemn music on the organ.

One spring evening, after ploughing with an old Fordson tractor he had bought, he was reversing it into the shed beside the house when he heard the scream above the shudder of the engine. He hadn't seen the wee girl playing in the shed. He ran with her in his arms along to Doctor Murdoch's house. She was still unconscious and the doctor said she would have to be sent to the mainland for examination. He and his wife sat up with her all night and he carried her down to his cabin on the steamer. An ambulance was waiting on the pier of the mainland town, but she had sustained head injuries which, the consultant warned, had left her with permanent brain damage.

'It was an accident. You weren't to know she was in the shed,' his wife tried to reassure him.

'I should have looked,' he kept repeating in his anguish.

Before, he had come straight home after the ferry was berthed for the night. Now he spent an hour in the bar of the Arms before he climbed the brae home. Ishbel noticed that he was unsteady on his feet as he came in, hanging his cap on the hook behind the door. He told her that he was late because it had been a 'rough crossing', but she knew that he had been in the Arms. As he was eating his supper the brain-damaged child was crawling at his shoes, making unintelligible sounds.

He began to criticise Ishbel's cooking, complaining that there was too much salt in the soup, or that there wasn't enough butter in the potatoes. One night he rose from the table and scraped the contents of his plate into the swill bin. She lay rigid with anxiety beside him in bed, with the knowledge that this wasn't the same gentle and considerate person who had waited for her to come off duty at the Hebridean Hotel and who had removed his heavy nautical coat and wrapped it round her to protect her from the icy blast from the Sound.

He had disposed of the tractor. One evening when he was scything the hay the boy wandered too close to the sweeping blade. Instead of cautioning him he dragged Ruari into the house, hauled down his trousers with such force that the buttons came away and thrashed him. Ishbel heard his screams and hurried through from the kitchen, to see the little boy, naked from the waist, crawling into a corner and curling up like a mortally wounded animal. She knew by the anguish in his eyes that he would never trust his father again.

'Why did you do that?' she rounded on him for the first time in their marriage.

'Because he got in the way of the scythe. I could have cut his legs to the bone.'

'You've done a lot more damage than that by thrashing him.'

He swore at her, snatched his jacket from the hook and slammed the door. When he came home hours later he stood swaying in the doorway. She was listening to a Gaelic talk on the radio and when he took a step towards her, his hand raised, she thought that she was about to receive the same as their son.

'I am truly sorry for what happened, Ishbel. I should not have done that to the boy.'

Though she saw the half bottle of whisky sticking out of his jacket pocket, she told him: 'I'm sure he'll get over it, John. I'll make us some tea.'

A week later he brought home a model steamer which he had bought on the mainland.

'We can sail it in the burn,' he told his son.

Ruari touched the red funnels, then turned back to the book he was reading.

'That cost me two pounds!'

'Leave him, John,' Ishbel pleaded. 'He wasn't feeling very well today. You like the boat that daddy bought you, don't you, Ruari?'

He heard the warning in his mother's voice and shut the

book. He carried the boat out to the burn that ran beside the house and launched it while his father watched. It swayed along, then ran under the bank.

'It's gone in for shelter!' his father called.

When the dark nights came in it was Ishbel's habit to go up to the window of their bedroom and watch for the mast lights of the ferry coming up the Sound. Throughout that November day the storm had strengthened until it was force nine. She lingered by the phone, expecting a call from the mainland port to tell her that the ferry couldn't make the crossing. But no message came and she assumed that it had sailed. It was due in at six o' clock, but she was still standing at the window at seven, with thoughts that the ferry had sunk in the Sound. When she went down to lift the phone to call the pier she found the line dead.

What was she going to do? She knew that she and the two children wouldn't be able to battle their way down to the town in the face of such force – especially when Sileas, the damaged one, was such a handful. It seemed that the storm was trying to wrench out the window she was standing at, praying that the ferry was safe. Perhaps it hadn't left the mainland, or perhaps it was sheltering further down the Sound.

She made herself tea then, having checked that the children were sleeping, she went back through to the window to resume her vigil, convinced now that the ferry hadn't left the mainland port. At midnight as the wind was abating she saw two mast lights moving slowly up the Sound and watched them turning into the bay. When he came up in his black oilskins streaming with rain, water dripping from the gold anchor on his peaked cap secured with a strap under his chin, she thought he looked majestic.

'Why did you leave the mainland in such weather?' she asked, as she served him food. He hadn't eaten on the ferry, all the plates in the pantry having been smashed in the storm.

But he couldn't explain to her that he had been sitting for part of the day drinking whisky in a bar while the wind whipped the water white in the bay outside and when he went round to the shipping office he told them that he would sail as usual. They didn't query his decision because they knew that he was a highly experienced seaman; what they didn't know was that he had been drinking and that taking a ship through such weather was a challenge to him, after having sailed the Sound on so many calm days, bored on the bridge. It was the same psychology, the same recklessness as the Lords of the Isles crossing to their Irish lands in their galley, a dozen muscular men rowing against the wind that couldn't be allowed to defeat them.

'We had to shelter in a bay for a few hours but we got through,' was all he told his wife as he drank tea and lit a cigarette.

He had created a legend on the island, with people down on Main Street huddled at their windows, certain that loved ones who were sailing on the ferry had perished in the storm, and instead of blaming Captain Henderson for his recklessness in sailing, they praised his seamanship.

But the following spring, on a day with little wind and an even sea, the ferry hit the pier. The Captain was on the bridge, directing the engine room, but on the sail up the Sound he had left the mate in charge on the bridge to go to the bottle in his cabin. Those standing on the pier heard the splintering sound as the bow sheared away several of the timbers.

'It wasn't my mistake,' he insisted to his wife when he went home, unsteady on his feet.

She daren't argue with him and the boy was watching warily as the plate of broth was placed in front of his father. Even the damaged daughter was subdued on the carpet, as if she understood that there was an explosive mix of whisky and anger waiting to be ignited.

At the formal enquiry, the engineer was able to convince the panel that he had carried out the orders he had received from the bridge. It was found that Captain John Henderson had been negligent, but since no doctor had examined him, it couldn't be proved that he had been drunk at the time and no crew member was willing to testify about his weakness. He was suspended for a month by the shipping company and given a formal warning.

Six months later his vessel demolished one of the piers in the Sound from which farmers loaded their cattle for shipment to mainland sales. An expensive bull plunged into the sea, bellowing as it drowned. The ferry was so badly damaged that it had to go to a Clyde yard for costly repairs, and a substitute boat sent for the island run. The Captain had to get a lift home on a fishing boat and appeared in the house at midnight without his cap.

'What on earth happened?' Ishbel asked fearfully.

'I made a slight misjudgement.'

'What do you mean?'

When he explained that the steamer had rammed a pier, she put her face into her hands.

'They'll dismiss you this time,' she warned him.

'I'm tired of the sea anyway. I'd like to spend some time ashore.'

'What are you going to do? The croft certainly won't support us.'

She daren't put into words what she was thinking: *who's going to give you a job on the island if you're taking drink?*

He held up a warning hand. 'I've had enough for one day, woman.'

'Woman? My name's Ishbel and I'm your wife. I've remained faithful to you even though it's evident to me that you have a drink problem.'

'Enough!' He brought his fist down on the table.

The letter accusing him of 'gross misconduct while in charge of one of the company's vessels' arrived three days later. 'You put passengers and crew in a state of fear and danger by issuing confused signals which caused the vessel to ram the pier and therefore we have no alternative but to dismiss you, since you were already on your final warning.'

He lay in his bed for several days and when he eventually rose his appearance frightened her. He was unshaven and his eyes were wild.

'Where are you going?' she asked as he pulled on a tweed cap.

'To look for work.'

By the following day John Henderson was catching the rope flung from the ferry and tethering it to a bollard as it came into the pier, with a new Captain on the bridge.

He helped one of the other stevedores to hoist the gangway, and went on board to assist the elderly off with their cases.

'Are you on leave, John?' an old woman returning from a stay with her daughter in Glasgow asked him in Gaelic. 'I was looking for you on the bridge.'

'I had a little bother,' he told her.

'I hope it's not serious,' she responded anxiously.

'It's very serious, Katie.'

Every evening the stevedores were paid in cash, but instead of taking the modest amount up the hill he went into the Arms.

'I hear they're selling the pier as matchsticks,' Dan MacAllister shouted up from one end of the bar to the line of habitual customers, their boots on the corroded brass rail.

John Henderson stood impassively, drinking whisky, but when the taunt was repeated he set down his glass carefully and went to his tormentor, catching him by the front of his jersey and practically lifting him out of his seaboots.

'One more word and I'll have to close your mouth for you,' he warned MacAllister, throwing him back against the bar.

'It was only a joke,' a voice protested.

'If anyone wants to come out on to the street with me, they'll see if I'm laughing,' the disgraced Captain invited. He fitted on his cap in the mirror, then walked with shoulders back towards the door. As he reached it an empty cigarette packet hit him on the back of the head. He hesitated, then pushed out into the night.

'You're drunk again!' Ishbel shouted at him when he came in.

'I stopped in the Arms for one.'

'For one? Where's the money you earned today?'

He put the ten shilling note on the table. She picked it up and inspected it as if it were a counterfeit.

'This won't go anywhere near to feeding four mouths. You drank the rest.'

All the way up the brae his anger had been gathering at the insults in the Arms. The girl was crawling at his feet, undoing his shoe laces. He picked her up roughly and dumped her on the sofa.

Murdo Maclean was walking up Bath Street in the November night, having been in the city to buy sheet music for the accordion when a voice spoke to him from a doorway.

'Have you any change?'

The medical student noticed that the cap between the beggar's shoes was a nautical one, with an anchor on the front. This, together with the accent, made him move so that he could see the man's face in the light from the street.

'It can't be Captain Henderson.'

There was no response as Murdo emptied the contents of his pockets into the cap. He was turning away when the figure spoke from the doorway.

'And who may you be?'

Murdo told him that he was the son of the island bank manager.

'Your father's a very fine man,' the voice said solemnly.

'So it is you, Captain.'

Returning to school on the mainland after a weekend at home, Murdo would look up to the bridge and see the Captain standing there in his white-topped cap, the anchor dazzling in the sun.

'No one has called me Captain for many years.'

'Why are you here?' Murdo asked, sitting beside him on the step, though it was so cold.

'I would have thought everyone on the island would know about the pier I had an unfortunate encounter with. I will say this, though, your father never criticised me once and was always very courteous to me. It was he who gave me the money to come to Glasgow to look for work and I'm afraid that I've never repaid the loan. Apologise to him from me. Tell him that John Henderson finds himself short of funds at present, but will send him a few pounds when he has it.'

'Where are you living?' Murdo enquired.

'Where I can find a corner. The Seamen's Institute on the Broomielaw's my home and when there isn't room for me, I make do with a doorway. What are you doing in Glasgow?'

'Studying medicine.'

'Ah well, if you're as clever as your father you'll make a big success of it. Where do you stay?'

'I'm in Maclay. It's a hall of residence.'

As he was speaking, Murdo opened his duffle coat and produced his wallet. He extracted a pound note and placed it in the nautical cap.

'That is another debt I owe to the Maclean family,' the disgraced Captain said.

They shook hands and Murdo went back to the Hall, but found he had no appetite for his supper, which Brogan beside him was pleased to eat, as he was always complaining about the sparse rations.

Murdo phoned his parents that night to tell him of his meeting on Bath Street.

'It's years since I've heard anything about him. I thought he had died,' his father told him.

'Did he become a down-and-out because he hit the pier?' his son asked.

'That was the reason he lost his job. But he ran over his daughter with the tractor and never forgave himself. Then he separated from Ishbel, a fine woman who made a great success of bringing up the children, considering that one of them is damaged.'

'He says he owes you money,' Murdo told his father.

'When I gave it to him out of my own pocket, since he would never have qualified for an overdraft because of his drinking, I never expected to see the money again. I gave it to him so that he could go to Glasgow to try to make a new life for himself. He told me that he had a place on a cargo boat, but I never learned the truth of it. So he's begging in the streets of Glasgow now. He must be very far down.'

'He seemed very sober when I was speaking with him.'

'That's a feature of alcoholics. They have to ingratiate themselves to get money for the next drink, and then they become insensible.'

'He tells me that he hangs about the Seamen's Institute,' Murdo informed his father.

'Son, I know you have a good heart, which is why you'll make an excellent doctor – if you can stay off the accordion long enough to attend to your medical studies. But John

Henderson has let himself go and it's probably too late to help him. I'll put your mother on.'

Some nights, as he huddled in the doorway on the Broomie-law, his face rimed with frost, bare feet in laceless shoes, he was back on the croft. His new daughter was playing with his hat, tracing the outline of the gold anchor with her tiny fingers.

'She's going to be a bright one,' Ishbel had predicted in Gaelic.

She had become unmanageable and was in an institution in the same city, propelling herself in an erratic wheelchair. Once he had stayed sober for two days, shaving in the Seaman's Institute and borrowing a blue serge suit so that he could go to see her, but his courage had failed him at the gates.

'Soup?' the female Samaritan said, her gloved hand holding out the cup on the freezing riverside street, but there was no response.

.

6. Lus

When he first arrived in Glasgow and was on duty in the vicinity, Seumas MacNiven had accepted Mary Ann Mackinnon's invitation to drop into Doig the bakers for some refreshment. Though it was three o' clock in the afternoon, she would insist that he ate a meal and would emerge from the kitchen with a plate heaped with two pieces of haddock and sufficient chips for two persons. She squeezed into the seat opposite him, as if she were watching a small boy she had ordered to clear his plate of food which he didn't like. Then she would go behind the counter and bring back the last cream horn which she had been saving for herself. When he protested that he had no more room, she told him in Gaelic: 'You can find a wee bit more space.' And she was gone again, this time returning with a pot of tea.

Seumas felt sick as he resumed his light duties. Because

he was a member of the police pipe band, he wasn't sent into the rough areas of the city but patrolled the centre, looking not for criminals, but for illegally parked cars. He decided not to go back into Doig's, but Mary Ann wasn't going to give up on a man she had taken a fancy to. When the pipe band was playing in one of the parks on a Sunday, she would take a bag of confections from her place of work together with a rug and a flask of tea for two in a basket and sit as close as possible to the pipers. Her applause was the loudest and as Seumas was folding his pipes into their box, she came up and took his arm, dragging him to her picnic. He felt self-conscious in front of his fellow band members as he sat on the rug, a napkin from Doig's spread on the lap of his kilt as Mary Ann fussed around, serving him sandwiches which she had cut into triangular shapes and then a selection of stolen cakes.

'Is that your sister?' one of the pipers asked him when they were in the bus.

'No, she's a friend.'

'She's a hefty lassie!' a voice from the back observed. 'You'll need to get a strong bed.'

'It's not like that, she's a friend,' Seumas insisted testily.

'Aye, she's feeding you up,' someone else remarked. 'I'm just wondering how many yards the wedding dress will take.'

Seumas was getting angry with Mary Ann's appearances at the band's performances, though he knew he couldn't stop her. Once when he refused the picnic on the excuse that he had a sore stomach, she came round to his lodgings in Ashley Street that night with a bag of green leaves which she proceeded to empty on to Mrs MacCaig's kitchen table.

'What's that?' the householder asked suspiciously.

'*Lus*.'

'What kind of *lus*?' Mrs MacCaig persisted. 'There are a lot of kinds of *lus*. Is it *lus a' bhainne* (milkwort) or *lus na macraidh* (wild thyme)? '

'I don't know what kind of *lus* it is,' Mary Ann answered. 'My mother sends it down from the island when I have a sore stomach.'

Mrs MacCaig wanted to say: *If you didn't eat so much of Doig's stock you wouldn't need to be taking any kind of lus.*

'It's for Seumas. He had a sore stomach at the piping this afternoon.'

Mary Ann bent down with considerable stress on the seams of her skirt and lifted out a pot from underneath the sink. She filled it with water and dunked the plants into it, placing it on the coals on the range. These seemed to burn continually, like a fire in the Hebrides that is smoored, because the kitchen was used for social gatherings as well as cooking and Mrs MacCaig was used to sitting up until the small hours, a glass in her hand. If it weren't full she was swinging it in time to the visitor singing a Gaelic song.

After half an hour of boiling and simmering, Mary Ann used a sieve to drain the liquid into a cup.

'What's that smell?' Seumas asked.

'Your medicine,' his landlady informed him.

When he looked apprehensive she added: 'Mary Ann said you had a sore stomach this afternoon and couldn't eat her picnic, so she came round with some kind of *lus* – she doesn't know what kind herself – to cure you.'

The young piper looked with extreme anxiety at the cooling glass of urine-coloured liquid.

'I'm not drinking that.'

But Mary Ann picked up the herbal preparation and held it to his mouth. He looked appealingly at his landlady but she was enjoying the entertainment enormously.

'Drink it up like a good boy!' she called out in Gaelic.

Seumas wanted to strike the glass out of the herbalist's hand, but he was intimidated by her size and authority, so he took the concoction. Even though he downed it in one draught it still tasted obnoxious and he wanted to retch into the stone sink.

'You'll be fine by the morning,' Mary Ann assured him.

But that night in the bed he shared with the restless undertaker, the young policeman felt very ill and spent the hours hurrying between the bed and the toilet. As he lay holding his stomach he wondered if Mary Ann had deliberately poisoned him because he had rejected her advances. By the morning he was no better and Mrs MacCaig phoned in to his station to say that he had a 'stomach upset.'

'I'm never going near that woman again,' he vowed to his landlady when he went through to the kitchen that evening in his dressing-gown, still feeling shaky, refusing her offer of a plate of herring.

'You're not going to get away from her so easily,' Mrs MacCaig warned him. 'If you don't go into the bakers for a feed she'll be round here with the food in a basket, or she'll be sitting there with it when you're playing with the band. She's in love with you.'

Seumas had thought the overweight manageress was being maternal and received his landlady's judgement with horror.

'Oh yes, that's easy to tell,' Mrs MacCaig persisted, having fun at the expense of her lodger.

'How the hell do I get rid of her?' he cried out.

'Well, I can hardly tell her not to come back here, because that wouldn't be hospitable and I like to keep an open house. It helps to keep my Gaelic going, you see, otherwise I would lose it. I know people who came to Glasgow with perfect Gaelic and within a very few years they couldn't pass the time of day with you in their native language because they'd lost it through not speaking it. Besides, Mary Ann's related to me. Her mother and I are cousins, so it would be a very big insult to turn the daughter away from my door, especially when she hasn't done anything to me. She was trying to be helpful, bringing round the *lus*, whatever kind it was. It didn't agree with you, maybe because you've got a delicate stomach.'

'Then I'm going to have to find other lodgings.'

Mrs MacCaig hadn't anticipated this. However, she was the kind of person who usually had an answer ready.

'Wherever you go to stay in this city – and I'd be very sorry to see you leave my house – she would still find you, in the same way as she makes it her business to keep in touch with those who come down to the city from the island. As I told you, she's in love with you and she's a persistent young woman, so wherever you go, she'll find you.'

'What am I going to do?' he appealed in despair.

'Well, I'd keep clear of Doig's, for a start. The more she sees you, the more she wants you. It's like cream horns.'

'I don't follow you.'

'Some nights she'll bring round a box of cakes with six cream horns in it, three for herself and three for me, and she sits there, stuffing herself because she can't resist them. I'm lucky if I get one. She's addicted to them in the same way as she's addicted to you.'

The image of being devoured by the overweight bakery manageress was too much for the young policeman.

'How am I going to get rid of her?' he repeated.

'Well, you don't want to give up playing with the pipe band, so as soon as you've finished playing you need to make yourself scarce.'

He saw himself fleeing across the park, his pipes bundled under his arm, being pursued by the stout woman with the basket of stolen confectionery, the other hand clamping on her straw hat.

'But she'll come round here,' he pointed out.

'That's the problem. You never know when she's going to appear. I often think it depends on the number of cakes she keeps back that day. It's certainly got nothing to do with the weather, because she's arrived here from New City Road soaking, dripping so much water that I've had to mop the floor after her. She doesn't go on the buses any more because she finds it difficult getting on and off, with her weight. I believe she fell off a tram once, in the Cowcaddens. She wasn't hurt, but they had to hold up the traffic till they got her on her feet again. It's a pity about her weight, because she's a bonny lass with a good heart.' She saw the expression on her lodger's face and added hastily: 'Of course she can be annoying, the way she presses food on people – especially food she hasn't paid for.'

'She's a thief,' Seumas said with uncharacteristic savagery.

'Well, that's a strong word you would usually use for the

type of people you have to deal with in the police – people who break into houses. I wouldn't say Mary Ann comes into that category. It's more that she wants to welcome people to the city by feeding them as soon as they arrive, then telling them to come in for a cup of tea and a cake even when they've settled in. She doesn't let people pay because she thinks they don't have enough money.'

But the young policeman couldn't accept this benevolent judgement. His profession made it clear that there was no moral distinction between holding up a bank and taking sixpence from someone's purse. Both were acts of theft, though on a different scale. What Mary Ann was doing in the bakers was embezzling from her employer. Tellers misappropriated cash from the banks they worked in, and she misappropriated cakes and plates of fish and chips. If he were doing his duty as a policeman – as he had been instructed at the police college – he should report her.

But there were problems to doing this. He himself was an accessory to the crime, having accepted meals and confections from her, knowing them to have been stolen. If he turned her in, she would tell his superiors that she had shared the cream horns with him and he would be dismissed from the force and from the pipe band and would have to return to the island to work the family croft, just when he was beginning to enjoy living and working in the city. What made him even more angry was that she had deliberately drawn him into her criminal activities by serving him stolen food, knowing that he couldn't turn her in.

The thought that his ethical standards as a policeman had been compromised made him feel sick. He was beginning to hate Mary Ann. But he knew, from his religious upbringing (his people were staunch adherents of the Free Church) that hatred was a sin and that one had to be forgiving and show tolerance. But his charity stopped at accepting Mary Ann Mackinnon as his girlfriend. For one thing, she was too fat. He found fat women ungainly. For another, she would surely damage his health by feeding him so much sugar, because he liked to keep fit and once a week went to a gymnasium. His father had been a noted wrestler in the Highland Games and had taught his young son how to throw an opponent and to keep them down. Seumas intended to use his fortnight's holiday during the Glasgow Fair to compete on the circuit of the Highland Games. A wrestler needed to be in prime condition, not with his blood saturated with sugar from cakes, making him sluggish and an easy throw.

'Maybe thief is too strong,' he conceded to his landlady. 'But I don't have any interest in her and I'm going to have to tell her.'

This decision was so delicate that it entailed Mrs MacCaig pouring herself another generous libation of whisky. She let it spread its benevolent warmth through her ageing body before advising this earnest young man.

'If you tell her straight, you'll hurt her very badly. She's a sensitive soul.'

'Will you tell her?' the lodger asked his landlady.

She was taken aback by his request, though she knew that the police often turned questions back on those they were interviewing.

'I don't think it's my place, Seumas. We're going to have to find a better way.'

'I need to get her off my back.'

As soon as he spoke the phrase, he realised how apt it was, considering his interest in wrestling. How did you throw an overweight opponent, something his father hadn't taught him?

'You're going to have to tell a wee white lie,' his landlady proposed.

Being a policeman committed to the truth, he looked shocked.

'Tell her that you've had a medical and that they've found a lot of sugar in your blood and you've been warned off sweet things. That'll stop her bringing you cakes.'

'But if she thinks I'm not well she'll bring more of that awful *lus*,' he pointed out in alarm.

'You can tell her that you've only to drink water.'

'But that won't stop her coming to this house.'

'No, I'm afraid it won't. But at least you won't have to eat cakes any more.'

Two nights later Mary Ann appeared in the flat with a box of cakes, but when she put a sugary bun on the plate for him he pushed it away, telling her that he'd had a medical from the police doctor and that he wasn't allowed sweet things any more.

The bearer of the stolen confections looked alarmed.

'Oh dear, I'm sorry to hear that. I'll write to my mother tonight.'

'Why would you do that?' Mrs MacCaig asked.

'Because she'll send me a *lus* that'll deal with sugar in the blood.'

'The doctor said I was only to drink water,' Seumas told her in a panic.

'He shouldn't take any kind of *lus*, because whatever's in it could disagree with him, and he could go into a coma,' the landlady cautioned.

'We can't have anything happening to you,' Mary Ann said earnestly. 'We'll have to find something else that will agree with you.'

She put her arms round him and for a moment Seumas feared that he was about to be carried to the bed he shared with the undertaker.

The following day Mary Ann informed the three other members of staff that she had a medical appointment and would be absent from the shop for an hour or so.

'Whatever you do, don't sell these three cream horns,' she warned them.

Instead of going to her doctor's she went to the Mitchell Library and asked for assistance. The woman brought her an armful of books and Mary Ann sat consulting them. On her way back to the bakers she went shopping.

'What happened to the three cream horns?' she demanded to know when she saw the empty glass shelf.

'I went and forgot and sold them,' the assistant apologised, winking at her colleague behind the manageress's bulky back.

'You sold them when I told you not to?' she declared indignantly.

'Yes. A Mrs Doig came in and said she was the wife of the owner and she bought the three cream horns and the four apple turnovers.'

Mary Ann, who was a trusting person, didn't realise that she was being lied to.

'A Mrs Doig, did you say? I hope she got good service.'

'Everyone gets good service who comes into this shop,' the assistant said defensively.

Mary Ann spent that evening in her old-fashioned kitchen in New City Road and the following evening appeared at Mrs MacCaig's with a box.

'But you were told that Seumas can't eat cakes any more,' the landlady said in alarm as she watched them being arranged on a plate.

'These are special cakes I made myself,' Mary Ann said proudly. 'They're sugar-free. I got the recipe from a book in the Mitchell Library.'

An hour later, when Seumas came in from duty, Mary Ann held the plate of cakes out to him, explaining that they couldn't harm his health. He looked a beaten man as he bit into the tasteless sponge.

7. Dishonour

The studious in their rooms in Maclay Hall raised their heads from their textbooks in engineering and Anglo-Saxon to listen to a clattering sound coming from the depth of the building. It wasn't a tradesman working late, but Tomás Murray practising Irish dancing. He had come to Glasgow to study medicine because of a photograph on his grandmother's mantelpiece in Cork. It showed two of his ancestors, the brothers Freddie and Willie Murray, wearing long-tailed dress coats and breeches and displaying the All-Ireland Belt they both won.

'Ireland never produced finer dancers,' Tomás's grandmother claimed. 'Freddie there – the one with the moustache – was a journeyman stonemason and travelled about a lot. When he laid down his tools in the evening he taught Cork dancing wherever he happened to be. He was in prison during the Troubles and men from as far away as Sligo and Galway learned to dance from him in the cells.

'It was said that the clatter of their boots on the stone almost put the guards off their heads. Freddie's setting of the Garden of Daisies is the one everyone dances – including myself as a young one. Willie went to London and taught the Cork style there. Willie won the All-Ireland Belt three times, and Freddie once,' the elderly woman recalled as her grandson ate a bowl of colcannon at her table. 'God knows where the belt is now, but the panels were silver, so it'll be worth a pretty penny. You could win it back for us Tomás if you eat up your colcannon and practise your steps.'

Every Saturday morning in the hall in Cork, Tomás beat out the steps of Three Sea Captains and other difficult set dances, an old man with rheumy eyes supplying the music from a vintage accordion. The teacher had a long cane and when Tomás put a foot wrong the cane would crack on the floor by his feet and he would have to begin again. When he was ten he crossed to Glasgow to dance in a competition in the Dixon Hall as part of a team, but he and the other Cork participants were up against formidable competition from the Peggy O'Neill Dancers who had medals sewn on to their jackets and precise steps. Nevertheless Tomás was commended for his slip jig.

Tomás (he insisted on the accent on the á because he was an Irish speaker) is dancing to a record in the basement of Maclay Hall, because he's in training for the All-Ireland Championship the following year. Already he has an impressive array of trophies and several dozen medals which his mother sewed lovingly on to a cloth and which he displays on the wall of his single study-bedroom in Maclay, beside the crucifix which he has affixed there and beneath which he kneels morning and evening, asking for the wisdom to become a doctor and the strength to become the All-Ireland Champion adult male dancer. His wardrobe space contains the saffron kilt he dances in and at the bottom, a selection of hard and soft dance shoes.

The pounding of his hard shoes is deplored by some of the residents of the Hall and appreciated by others. The studious studying bridge construction and Sweet's Anglo-Saxon Reader found it distracting, but Brogan the rugby prop kept time to the beat below with his brogue as he read the sports pages of the Herald.

It didn't bother Murdo Maclean. In fact as he practised his accordion in the music room he found that at times the beat was like a double bass backing up the reel he was playing. Besides, he had made friends with Tomás because of their mutual interest in music and dance, as well as medicine.

Tomás went regularly to the *ceilis* held by the Irish community in Glasgow, who danced a sixteen-hand reel unique to that city. Children with confident steps would be on the floor, because those who had fled the potato famine in Ireland the previous century had been determined to keep their culture alive in the Glasgow slums they called home. The soft shoes performing in time to the fiddle in the stinking entrance to the tenement would have been made with love on an Irish last.

On the first day that the Pakistani student appeared in the lecture theatre there were gasps from some of the males who had still to learn how to treat women courteously, as well as to deal with patients. Her name was Malika (meaning queen). Her shining black hair fell to her shoulders and her figure was wrapped in a white robe trimmed with gold. As she listened attentively to the lecture Tomás was watching her, and by the time the chemistry of the blood had been explained he was in love with her. That evening his dancing in Maclay seemed to pace his heart.

Two days later he chose a seat further down the tiers in the lecture theatre and when she left he slipped out behind her.

'Would you like a coffee?' he asked in his Irish accent.

She turned and looked at him in surprise, the teeth in her smile almost dazzling him.

'That's very kind of you,' she said in the mellifluous undulating tone he would come to adore.

Many students frequented the University Café on Byres Road run by the Verrecchia family since the last year of the First War. In the Second, when Italy entered on the side of Germany in 1940, the windows of cafés in Glasgow were shattered with bricks and their owners interned. But come peace-time the cafés had re-opened and sophisticated coffee machines were installed. The two medical students sat opposite each other, cradling cups in their hands as they each told their history. A decade before, her parents and five children had arrived in Britain because of the turbulence in the new state of Pakistan, forerunners of the substantial migration to come. Her father had worked for sixteen hours in a Glasgow warehouse to save enough money to put down as rent for a small shop.

'We all helped in it after school and at weekends,' Malika reminisced to Tomás. 'I was the only one of the five children who could reach the top shelves to stock them. But my father wasn't satisfied. He wanted bigger premises and when a more spacious shop came up for rent on New City Road, he had enough money to take it. It's one of the busiest shops in the city. Our customers are mostly white people from the tenements and my father keeps his prices affordable. My two brothers and sister are working in the shop now. My other sister's at college, learning how to keep accounts and she'll join the family business, because my father's determined to take on two other shops, one for each of my brothers.'

'And you've become a medical student,' Tomás said.

'Only after much opposition,' she told him earnestly, leaning over the table as if inviting him to bestow a kiss on irresistible lips.

'But surely your parents are proud of what you've achieved,' he pointed out.

'It's not a question of pride, but of religious beliefs. My parents are devout Muslims. Do you understand what that means?'

'I don't know anything about Muslims.'

'My father didn't want me to become a doctor because he said I would have to examine male patients intimately.'

'So how did you get round him?' Tomás asked.

'I had to pledge that I would become a doctor for females only – in other words, a gynaecologist. Now I have told you my story: what is yours?'

He explained that he came from County Cork and that his ancestors had been Irish dancers of distinction and freedom fighters for Ireland in the time of the Civil War, with guns hidden in the roof spaces of their humble abodes.

'Why are you not studying in Ireland?' she enquired.

He told her about his boyhood visit to Glasgow in an Irish dance team and how he had fallen in love with the city.

'I'd like to see you dance,' she said.

'There's a competition a fortnight Saturday. Why don't you come?'

'What time is it at?'

'It's on all day. I'll be dancing in the afternoon.'

'We can talk about it after classes tomorrow,' she told him, rising and lifting her books. 'I must go. If I'm not home by five my father gets angry.'

The following day after the chemistry lecture he repeated his invitation to the Irish dance competition.

'I could meet you at twelve and we could take a bus across to the south side,' he suggested.

'All right. But I'll have to be home by five.'

'Even on a Saturday?' he queried.

'That's the rule. I'll have to say I'm going to the library to study.'

He was to dance the Blackthorn Stick, and he practised each evening in his hard shoes in Maclay until even Brogan began to complain about the racket.

'How can I take in these difficult medical terms, with a bloody Paddy clattering away below?'

Tomás met Malika at noon on the Saturday at the fountain outside the Grand Hotel at Charing Cross and they travelled across to the church hall on the south side. He draped his dance costume over the empty seat beside him. The hall was crowded with competitors, some of whom had crossed from Ireland with their parents. Malika was enchanted with the apparel of the females; simple coloured dresses with shoulder-to-waist shawls embroidered with intricate Celtic designs; berets with feathers. The males, like Tomás, were in saffron kilts and jackets adorned with medals.

Malika sat in the front, giving the same concentration to the competitions as she did to her medical studies. When it was Tomás's turn she clapped him on to the stage and as he danced the Blackthorn Stick he kept his eyes on her lovely face. He felt perfectly relaxed, his arms straight by his sides. As he crossed the stage he seemed at times to take off and at the end he was presented with the medal. She held it in her hand on the bus home.

'Why don't we go and get something to eat?' he suggested.

'I would like to, but I must be home by five.'

'Can we go for a walk next Saturday?' he requested.

He arranged to be at the gate into Kelvingrove Park below Maclay Hall at one on the Saturday afternoon. He put on his sports jacket, flannels and the undergraduate tie that he had bought and was at the gate into the park at twelve thirty. She appeared, dressed in white pantaloon trousers, as the clocks of the city were striking the hour.

'What did you do this morning?' he asked as they walked the path.

'I worked behind the counter of the shop until twelve so that my mother could go and do errands. What did you do?'

'I practised my dancing.'

'I don't dance, but I like to sing,' she informed him.

'Would you sing for me just now?'

'I've never sang to anyone before,' she said shyly. 'I sing to myself.'

'Please sing for me,' he pleaded.

'But you don't understand Urdu.'

She stopped under a tree and began to sing in a thrilling voice that was like a caress to him.

'What's the song about?' he wanted to know.

'It's about the beauty of the world, the birds and the flowers.'

His time with her seemed to go in far too quickly, and when she was gone on her swift light feet across the bridge he sat disconsolately on a bench. In the evening when he should have been concentrating on the textbook in front of him he sat at the window of his room overlooking the park, wondering at which of the lighted windows in the city his beloved was studying. Every day after classes they went down to the University Café to drink coffees and to discuss their lives. She explained that her father belonged to the *Vaishyas* caste, that of a trader, and that he expected the same dedication and discipline from his family as he practised, going out in his van before dawn to buy produce in the Fruit Market, so that his customers would have fresh oranges and apples on their way to school or work. He refused to sell fireworks to children.

The residents of Maclay Hall were allowed to have female visitors at certain times and her appearance in the common room caused a sensation. Even Brogan removed his feet from the coffee table and came up to welcome his fellow classmate, and soon she had a group of admirers around her, including Murdo Maclean.

'You must come again to see us,' Murdo urged her, and when she had gone, they turned to Tomás. 'You're a lucky bugger, with a beauty like that. All the medics are jealous.'

That night his hard shoes seemed to fill the massive Hall with their beat and the following Saturday, when it was wet, he invited her into the Hall. He had bought a cake and had a flask of tea and two cups on a tray in the common room.

'Would you like to see my room?' he proposed.

'Is it allowed?'

'Oh yes.'

She looked at his desk with the pile of textbooks and asked him why he didn't move it to the window.

'Because it's a distraction, the view is so wonderful. I sit at the window at night and look out at the lights and I wonder: which is Malika's window? Is she studying or thinking of me?'

'Both,' she confessed with a light laugh.

He had her in his arms and when he kissed her mouth he met no resistance.

'I shouldn't have allowed you to do that.'

'It's nothing to be ashamed of. I love you and I hope that the feeling's returned.'

'I need to go home,' she told him.

There was a party in the Hall before the University broke up for the Christmas vacation. Females were invited, but as they were sitting in the University Café, Malika told Tomás that she couldn't attend. It was bitterly cold and she was wearing a blue cashmere wrap round her neck.

'Why can't you come to the party?'

'Because I'm not allowed out at night.'

'Surely you could ask permission just this once.'

'It wouldn't be granted.'

'But you could get a taxi to the Hall and back,' he said, bewildered. 'You wouldn't come to any harm.'

'My parents don't approve of parties. I'm sorry, Tomás, I would love to come, but it's not possible. When I'm studying I'll be thinking of you having a good time.'

'Then at least come to the Hall for tea on the afternoon of the dance.'

The residents had helped the staff to loop paper chains between the elegant cornices of the public rooms. Malika loved the tree, gold and silver baubles dangling from the branches, an angel with spread wings on top.

A large bowl of punch had been made by the students and Tomás ladled two portions into a saucepan and asked one of the staff to heat it up. He carried the steaming mugs up to his room. His present to her was lying on the bed. She untied the ribbon with her long nails and gently eased open the festive paper, uncovering a box. When she opened it she found a silver locket, with the inscription: *from Tomás to Malika with fondest love*.

'It's beautiful but I can't wear it. If my parents see it they'll stop me going out.'

'Then it's finished,' he said, turning away to the window.

'Why is it finished?' she wanted to know.

'Because I hardly ever see you and your life's dictated by your parents, though you're a grown woman.'

'Surely we can still be friends,' she pleaded.

He turned and took her in his arms. Downstairs, Murdo Maclean was practising his accordion for the dancing that would take place in the common room, its carpet rolled up.

Tomás laid her gently on his bed and lifted her dress.

'You have no protection,' she warned him, gripping his wrist.

But his hand was already caressing.

'We should not have done it,' she said afterwards, when she was adjusting her clothes.

'Why not? We love each other. I want to marry you, Malika.'

'My parents will never allow that. They expect me to marry one of our own caste. In fact they've chosen someone for me already.'

'Who is this man?' Tomás asked incredulously.

'He's a businessman in Glasgow. His family came to Glasgow ten years ago and now have four shops and other business interests. He drives a big car, and he's twenty years older than I am.'

'It doesn't sound as if you want to marry him.'

'I don't. But Pakistani parents believe they have the right to choose husbands for their daughters.'

'It's a heartless tradition,' Tomás argued heatedly. 'It doesn't take any account of love. We'll get married before we finish our medical studies because I don't want to wait that long. We'll present your parents with a *fait accompli*.'

'I don't think that would be wise,' she cautioned. 'You'll also have my two brothers to deal with.'

'Why should I be frightened of them?'

'Because they're very protective of me, and like my parents, they want me to marry someone of my own race and caste, as they will themselves.'

'Is this what you want, to have your life and your feelings dictated by other people?' he challenged her. 'I love you, and

I know you love me. I won't give you up to another man you've no interest in.'

'I must go, Tomás.'

He caught her wrist. 'Phone your parents and tell them you've met a friend at university. Tell them you won't be home till later. You can stay for the party.'

'I can't,' she told him.

'Do you love me?' he demanded, still holding her wrist.

'Yes I do.'

'Are you going to give me up?'

She shook her head and he released her wrist. He took her downstairs and phoned for a taxi because it was so cold and she was wearing flimsy garments. When she had gone he was disconsolate and didn't feel like going to the party. Instead he went down to the basement and sat on the floor with his back to the wall, without putting on his dance shoes.

He wouldn't see her the following week at classes because it was the Christmas vacation. Malika came round to Maclay on the Saturday afternoon. He had heated the room with an electric fire borrowed from one of the staff, and had a kettle with tea and cake for her. Afterwards they went to bed, her garments draped over the chair. Her back was to him and she seemed pensive, lying with her head on her arm, looking out of the window.

'How will you spend Christmas Day?' he asked.

'We don't celebrate Christmas. It'll be a normal day with the shop open. I'll serve behind the counter for a few hours.'

'Have you thought about what I said about us getting married?' he asked.

'It's too soon to talk about that. The medical course is a long one.'

He wasn't satisfied with that answer, but decided not to force the issue. That evening he walked down to Charing Cross and along New City Road. He didn't know the number of her family's shop, but was looking for open premises. There were far fewer Asian shops than there would be a decade later. He came to a shop on the corner and looked in the window. A man was sitting on a stool behind the counter, reading a book.

Tomás went home across the Irish Sea to a festive season of Masses and *ceilis* in which he danced, but he was preoccupied with thoughts of his sweetheart in Glasgow and made elementary mistakes in his footwork. He took the boat back to Glasgow on the third day of January. When Malika didn't turn up at the Hall the following Saturday, as arranged, he was worried and hung around the phone, hoping for a call. The rest of the vacation was miserable and he didn't dance. He was up at the university early on the first day of the new term, but she wasn't in classes. He decided to go to the medical secretary.

'Is Malika ill?' he asked her.

'I haven't had any notification.'

He went round to the shop in New City Road that evening.

'Are you Malika's brother?' he asked the young man sitting behind the counter.

'Yes. What's your name?'

'Tomás Murray. I'm in the same medical year as your sister.'

'She isn't well just now, but I'll tell her you're asking for her.'

'What's wrong with her?' he asked anxiously.

'A woman's complaint.'

'Can I see her?'

He shook his head. 'She isn't well enough, but she can send you a message. Where do you live?'

'The Maclay Hall of residence.'

'Where's that?'

Tomás gave its location.

'Tell her I send my love and hope to see her soon,' he said as he went out.

At the end of the month there was an Irish festive dance in the same hall in which Malika had sat watching him taking the medal for the Blackthorn Stick. He didn't want to go because he was anxious about Malika, but he had agreed to do a solo turn in the interval between the set dances, when the colcannon, which had been made at home and brought to the hall in large pots, was served.

'I forgot to bring my hard shoes,' Tomás told the priest who was selling raffle tickets from a stitched-up apron round his waist.

'That doesn't matter. Dance in the shoes you're wearing, and the Good Lord will see you through.'

But his feet seemed uncoordinated and he made elementary mistakes.

'You'll have to do better than that if you're to win the All-Ireland,' a man warned him when he came off the platform.

But the All-Ireland was the last thing in his thoughts. The following morning he went to church half an hour before Mass was due to begin. It was empty, except for an old woman in a mantilla sitting saying her rosary, its beads clicking against the pew. Tomás lit a candle at the blazing rack for his lover, then went down on his knees in front of the altar and prayed that she would be restored to his arms soon.

When he returned to the Hall there was an envelope waiting for him.

Can you meet me tonight at 9pm at the fountain outside the Grand Hotel? Love, Malika.

He ate his supper in the company of Murdo Maclean.

'I notice that Malika hasn't been at classes. Is she not well?'

'She's been ill, but is better now. I'm meeting her tonight outside the Grand,' Tomás told his friend excitedly.

'It's raining,' Murdo pointed out.

What did that matter when he was meeting his beloved? He turned up the corner of his coat as he hurried down to the appointed rendezvous. He was sheltering in a doorway at the Grand Hotel, with the fountain in sight when two men came up to him. They were wearing western clothes, with caps pulled down.

'You're waiting for Malika?' one of them enquired.

'Yes. Is there something wrong?' asked anxiously.

'She asked us to take you to her,' one said.

He went with them along St George's Road, but before reaching New City Road they turned into a side street.

'In here,' Tomás was instructed, and followed them into a close. One of them closed the door and in the dim lighting lifted back his cap to reveal the face of her brother, the one Tomás had spoken with in the family store.

'Our sister can't see you.'

'Is she very ill?' Tomás asked.

'Not ill. Dishonoured.'

'What do you mean?'

The other brother spoke.

'Our father allowed our beautiful sister to go to study medicine at university on condition that she didn't mix with male students. But one of them pestered her and took her to his room where he seduced her and made her pregnant.'

The door of the close was shut. But Tomás loved Malika too much to try to get away.

'I want to marry her,' he told them earnestly.

'You hear that?' one turned to the other. 'A white man – and a Catholic – wants to marry our sister, a Pakistani and a Muslim.'

'It isn't allowed,' the other said, shaking his head solemnly.

'The problem is, she's pregnant, so the man from our own race who was going to marry her is no longer interested in her,' the first one spoke again. 'That's very unfortunate because we liked him, and because he would have brought money to develop our business. So what do we do now?'

The other brother opened his coat, to reveal the pick handle he was carrying. One twisted Tomás's arms up behind his back while the other set about him with the length of wood.

'Not my legs!'

But they ignored his pleas.

When they had asked their sister if this man Tomás Murray who had come to their shop was the one who had seduced her, she had refused to answer.

'If you don't tell us we'll kill you because you've dishonoured our family.'

'Kill me!' she screamed at them.

Instead they ransacked her room, finding the silver locket with his pledge of love.

'Not my legs!'

He was a champion Irish dancer and perfect balance was essential for the swift intricate steps. He knew that he could take the title at the All-Ireland and be as great a dancer as his ancestors the Murray brothers. He might even delight his ailing grandmother by winning back the belt with the silver panels which they were wearing in their photographs on her walls.

He heard the crack of his bones as the pick axe handle was laid about his legs and when he sank to his ruined knees they dragged him out of the close and dumped him in the gutter in the rain.

8. Asti Spumante

Almost everyone coming to Glasgow from the island had to arrive in Buchanan Street train station – unless they took the bus, but that was a longer journey along the shores of Loch Lomond. Ealasaid MacAllister arrived in the early evening, carrying her case. She had travelled on the first train she had seen in her nineteen years and in the station she inspected the rows of entertainment. In a glass case there were two opposing football teams, dressed in different colours of knitted woollen jerseys and white shorts. You put a penny in the slot, turned a knob and the ball appeared out of a hatch in the centre of the pitch. You made the players kick by pressing down a handle. When you scored, the ball disappeared down a hole behind the beaten goalkeeper.

But Ealasaid wasn't interested in football. She put a penny into the slot of the adjacent machine and laid her palm on the rows of buttons. They began to vibrate and then a card popped out of a slot. Ealasaid shook her head when she read that she was 'intelligent and would go far in her chosen career.'

She had worked in the scullery of the Hebridean Hotel above the bay on her native isle and the piles of pots and dishes on the board beside her never seemed to diminish. This was the age before rubber gloves became common and Ealasaid's hands became raw with the coarse soap and the constant scrubbing. There was a yacht race from the mainland once a year and on this particular night in July there were so many boats in the bay that the crews could walk ashore across the decks. But Ealasaid can't see them in the bay below through her steamed-up window. Her wispy auburn hair is sticking to the sweat on her face, her hands submerged under the scum. The dining-room is full of boisterous yachtspeople who have left their yellow boots and jackets piled in the hall, under the picture of a windjammer braving heaving seas. Ealasaid is close to tears because she knows that those next door will go on eating and drinking until eleven o' clock and it will be close to midnight when the last plate or utensil leaves her sink and she will practically crawl to her home above the town, only to have to rise at six to be up in the hotel in time for the first breakfast dishes coming through from the dining-room.

Ealasaid is scouring a burnt pot when she feels a pair of hands round her waist and she's practically lifted out of her flat functional shoes. Carlo is standing there, grinning. He's one of four waiters hired from a staff agency in Glasgow and flown over to Scotland from Italy. The proprietor of the hotel, a stout man who's addicted to cigars and West Highland terriers, likes to employ Italian waiters because they look good and are swift and efficient in the dining-room, able to carry plates up their arms without spillage. They talk seductively to the women who occupy the same single rooms overlooking the sea for a fortnight each summer and who, on an Italian recommendation, will risk a glass of wine. When they ascend the staircase (there is no lift) to their rooms they will giggle as they undo their suspenders and roll down their stockings, and when their girdles are draped over the backs of chairs, and they've said their prayers, they will dream of the dark handsome youth in the black waistcoat and tight black trousers who brought them their devils on horseback as if it were a dangerous choice.

'Leave me alone, Carlo,' Ealasaid warns him.

'You are very bootiful,' he tells her, taking a cigarette end from his waistcoat pocket and snapping open a lighter in which a naked woman is posing in the transparent tank of fuel.

'Don't annoy me.'

'There's a party at the staff quarters behind the garage and I would like that you would come. *Si?*'

No one has ever invited Ealasaid to a party, except when she was a child and was taken by the hand by her mother to the Sunday School party where they sang hymns before being served jelly and ice cream.

'I have to get up in the morning, Carlo.'

'So do I. So does everyone in the world,' he gestures impatiently. 'So what?'

'Get a move on, Carlo,' Bella the head waitress orders him. 'You've got number nine table to serve.'

Carlo is like a conjurer. The smoking cigarette is nicked and disappears into his waistcoat and the other hand produces a corkscrew.

'See you at the back door at eleeven,' he whispers to Ealasaid.

She plunges her hands into the greasy water and attacks the submerged pot, so that it is dredged up, gleaming. The pile of dishes on the board beside her begins to get smaller and soon there are none left, but at ten minutes to eleven the last table is cleared and cups and saucers are dumped down beside her. She completes these in eight minutes, lifts off her apron and clatters down the stone stairs. She's not a graceful girl because her legs are rather heavy and last year she went over her ankle on these stairs and was off for three days.

At the back door she sees the glow of her suitor's cigarette. He gives her a cuddle and leads her up the road to the staff quarters. He has under his jacket a bottle of Asti Spumante which he filched from the cellar when the proprietor (who, wisely, won't give out the keys to his staff) was stooping to pull an order from another bin. The three other Italians are in the staff quarters, with three girls from the town, and a portable record player is playing a Mario Lanza record in Carlo's bedroom, because there is no common room for the foreign workers. Carlo shakes the stolen bottle of sparkling wine, easing the cork off with his thumbs until it pops and strikes the ceiling. He pours the foaming wine into a glass and because she's not used to alcohol (her parents are strict teetotallers, so this is actually a sin in their book) when she swallows the Asti Spumante it travels to her head and Carlo's cluttered bedroom begins to tilt, giving her the impression that Christ hanging on His crucifix beside a poster of Sophia Loren is about to topple down the actress's formidable cleavage.

Later, a sober and contrite Ealasaid tries to reconstruct the sequence of events. She vaguely remembers dancing with the Latin round his bed, and then she seemed to fall on it, and he on top of her.

Ealasaid was very late home that night and had to ascend the staircase that her grandfather had made with his own hands. She was carrying her flat ugly shoes and once in bed, she dreamt of the promised matrimonial home in that far country. Three mornings later, when she went up to her sink in the Hebridean Hotel, she waited for her lover to emerge from the dining-room.

'Is Carlo not well?' she asked Bella anxiously.

The head waitress was going backwards through the swing door into the dining-room, a cloth in each hand grasping the hot plates of full English breakfasts.

'He left on the ferry to go home to Italy because his mother's ill. The boss doesn't believe the bugger.'

'Why not?' Ealasaid asked disconsolately.

'He thinks he arranged with someone in Italy to send the telegram because he was fed up here. The boss is angry because he's had to pay his air ticket home, without getting a full season's work out of him. That's foreigners for you.'

Ealasaid didn't believe the prediction on the card that had been delivered to her in Buchanan Street Station after she had laid her hand on the little knobs of the fortune telling machine. She picked up her case and went out into the overcast day. As she crossed the street a bus came towards her and the conductress leaned out and yelled: 'You could have got yersel killt, ye silly bitch!'

Ealasaid was close to tears as she went down the street. She had no idea where she was going, but she knew that she had to keep moving. She had missed her period for the first time ever, but didn't have the courage to go up the brae to Dr Kenneth Murdoch's consulting room in his villa among trees occupied by raucous rooks to ask him to confirm her pregnancy, because she was frightened that he would tell her parents. She had been a very late baby. Her elderly parents were both fiercely devout and on Sunday evenings when she had the Sabbath off from her duties in the hotel, and when other members of Ealasaid's generation were watching television in the town, she had to sit for an hour while her father read from the Gaelic Bible. Once she had nodded to sleep and her mother had kicked her on the ankle.

Because she couldn't subject them to the shame of having a baby out of wedlock she decided to leave the island. After giving her mother money for her keep each week, she had saved ninety pounds, enough to take her to Glasgow. What did she intend to do when she reached there? Get rid of the baby? But Ealasaid had never heard the Gaelic phrase *torrachas anabaich*, far less its English equivalent, abortion. She had even been ignorant of the anatomy of the male until Carlo had fired her curiosity with the stolen sparkling wine and the skill of his fingers. Here she was in Glasgow, having put as much distance as she could afford between herself and her parents, for on that morning she left home, they had found a letter written in poor English lying on her stripped bed, explaining that she was tired of island life and wanted 'to go to the mainland for a change.' It was nearing the end of the season and she didn't feel that she was letting down the proprietor of the Hebridean Hotel because she had given him such good service.

She was in Glasgow and the tall buildings on either side of her looked terrifying as she lugged her case down Buchanan Street. When she came to an intersection she set down her burden. A policeman standing near was watching her and approached her. When he spoke to her in Gaelic she was surprised; amazed, in fact, because it was the distinctive dialect of her own island. He asked her in their native language where she was going and she answered truthfully that she didn't know. Had she a job? No. Had she island friends in the city? No. He picked up her case. Was he taking her to the police station? But she hadn't committed any crime. She was pregnant because a suave Latino had stolen her virginity in the same way he had taken the bottle of Asti Spumante. It had not been love but lust.

The policeman knew an innocent young woman when he saw one, especially from the drab way in which she was dressed. Females three times her age were wearing these flat shoes, and the coat she was in had been fashionable twenty years before. It was the early 1960s, and the era of young liberation had begun. This same policemen had seen teenagers walking with their mini skirts round their waists on windy days in the city, as proud of their coloured knickers as they were of their long faultless legs. But this one, walking beside him, couldn't be more than twenty, yet looked much older. He would have taken her to Doig's, to leave her in the care of

Mary Ann, but the bakery was shut.

'We'll get you a room in here,' he told Ealasaid, stopping at a large building in Bath Street.

'What's this place called?' she asked apprehensively.

'This is the YWCA.'

'What does that stand for, sir?'

'The Young Women's Christian Association.'

The policeman opened the door for her. He left her with her case while he went to speak to the receptionist, who happened to be part of the Gaelic network of the city. The receptionist looked across to Ealasaid and nodded and minutes later she was being taken upstairs to a bedroom.

'Are you looking for work in the city?' the receptionist, whose name was Mabel, asked sympathetically.

'Yes.'

'What kind of work?'

'Anything. I've been washing dishes in a hotel since I left school. I want to do something different.'

Can you type?'

'No miss.'

'Have you ever worked in an office?'

'No miss.'

'Then we'll find you work in a hotel, dear – something better than washing dishes. You have a wee rest after your long journey, Ealasaid, and when I go off duty at five I'm going to take you down to a friend of mine at the Grand Hotel.'

Her name was Ina, and she was a waitress and another Gael. She spent her day off teaching Ealasaid how to carry plates and later, took her to a hairdresser and then to a clothes shop where the fledging waitress spent precious pounds of the savings she had brought from the island, clutching her bag on the train as if bandits would board at the next stop.

'I've spoken to the head waiter and you'll report for work at eight o' clock on Friday morning, so that you can see how we do breakfast.'

Ealasaid went back to her room in the YWCA, examined her shorn hair in the mirror and knew that it was an improvement, as were the two dresses she had bought. That night, having the luxury of her first bath in that quiet building, she saw the water redden. After she had towelled herself she said a Gaelic prayer of gratitude on her knees by the bedside.

On the Friday morning Ealasaid took a bus down to the Grand Hotel at Charing Cross. When she went in the front door, she was directed to the staff entrance by an abrupt porter. The head waiter, an elegant Scotsman, assigned a couple of tables to the new waitress. Ealasaid knew that she dared not make a mess, and wrote clearly on her pad the order for a kipper each for the elderly couple, the man in a three-piece tweed suit, the woman in a costume from an earlier era. Ealasaid carried the two hot plates in the napkin, as she had been shown in the tutorial and she was very careful when setting down the silver-plated pots of tea and coffee on the table, though the handles were hot in her hands. As instructed, she stood vigilantly, watching the two tables for a signal for more toast or marmalade.

'You did very well,' the head waiter complimented her when they were having breakfast in the staff hall. 'I'm going to increase your responsibility to four tables tomorrow morning and if all goes well, I'll put you on lunch duty.'

Now that she had the geography of the city centre in her

head, Ealasaid walked up via Sauchiehall Street to the hostel, stopping at the window of Richard Shops, shocked at the brevity of the skirts on display. On the island her mother would never have allowed her to buy a skirt that ended above her knee, had such a style been available, because the shop which sold women's garments was always at least ten years behind the prevailing fashion. How could young women walk about in these without showing their underwear?

Ealasaid was happy in the hostel. The young woman in the adjacent room was studying to become a missionary in India and at supper she told Ealasaid of the great need there was to spread the Christian message in the subcontinent, where, she had been told by her tutor, bullocks roamed in the streets of the cities and a gilded god was worshipped.

'But suppose they don't want to be converted?' Ealasaid asked.

Martha looked shocked, as if Ealasaid had uttered a profanity.

'They need to be converted, to be brought to the light of the true God. I know it can be dangerous; female missionaries have been violated.'

'What does that mean?' Ealasaid asked.

Her dining companion looked at her to satisfy herself that this was genuine interest.

'Women are ravished.'

But ravished was not a word known to Ealasaid.

'I mean, they're sexually attacked.'

'Why would you put yourself in such danger?' Ealasaid asked, horrified.

'Because the word of the Lord must be brought to them

to enlighten them,' Martha said, chanting the mantra she had learned from one of the tutors, an elderly man with flowing white hair who looked like a prophet from a biblical engraving.

Though Ealasaid admired the zeal and purity of the speaker, she did wonder if God would demand such a sacrifice. Though she considered herself a sinner for having lain with the Italian waiter, she believed that there was the possibility of forgiveness, because Carlo had seduced her, having first made her drink stolen wine. Surely it was God's benevolent intervention that she hadn't become pregnant.

She found that serving four tables at breakfast was easy, provided that when she went into the kitchen she picked up the correct food for the table which had ordered it. Replenishing tea pots and toast racks took all her attention until the last table was vacated and she could go to the staff hall for her own breakfast.

'I'm going to try you out on lunches today,' the head waiter informed her as he presided at the top of the table, smoking a cigarette.

'What does that involve?' Ealasaid asked fearfully.

'We have customers – mostly men – who come in for lunch every day. Some of them actually order the same courses – soup and steak pie – every day, so you should soon get into the way of things. People take longer over lunch than they do over breakfast, so in many ways it's easier. The one thing you have to watch out for is that someone else doesn't take their table, because some of them have had the same table for far longer than I've been here.'

Ealasaid was assigned two tables to begin with. They both belonged to regular customers and at half past twelve precisely the first of them came in. He was a stockbroker in the city exchange. Charles Straven was in his late forties and all his life had known privilege and comfort because his father had been a stockbroker before him, so successful that he had been able to acquire a fifty acre estate with a notable mansion house with a lodge at Kilmalcolm. Charles had been educated at Loretto School and had learned the basics of stockbroking with a London firm before joining his father in Glasgow. His office in Exchange Square had a leather-topped desk at which Lord Kelvin was reputed to have made some of his most inspired calculations in engineering.

Charles Straven's firm (of which he is senior partner) had always invested in traditional stocks such as mining and railways, but his niece Amanda, who had been staying with him recently, had changed things. As he ascended the stairs of his father's mansion to bed in the evening, Straven heard music throbbing through the stout door of the room Amanda was occupying for the weekend. Instead of knocking sharply to ask her to turn down the volume, he stood listening. It wasn't his type of music – he had a season ticket to opera in London – but he found himself tapping his handmade shoe on the sanded boards of the landing. At breakfast the following morning he asked his niece what she had been listening to.

'Cliff Richard and The Shadows singing "The Young Ones,"' she informed him.

'Interesting,' was his comment as he decapitated his egg with a silver spoon.

Straven wasn't interested in the music, but in its investment possibilities and that morning he asked his assistant to investigate the new music market. He went to lunch in the

Asti Spumante

Grand Hotel and encountered the new waitress, obviously nervous, the way she set down beside him the glass and bottle of Malvern water, which, he had instructed her, he always drank with his lunch, but without the vulgarity of ice. He also told her that his choice of steak pie never varied and that it was always followed by apple charlotte.

'Where are you from?' he questioned the new waitress.

When she told him the name of the island, he revealed that he sailed into its principal bay every summer and always dined in the Hebridean Hotel. She didn't tell him that she must have washed his dirty dishes in the stone sink of the steaming scullery where she had seen her own exhausted face in the bottoms of so many pots and pans.

When she went through to the kitchen of the Grand Hotel to collect the order, Ealasaid expressed the opinion to the chef that it was strange, a customer eating the same fare, day in, day out.

'It suits me,' the chef informed her. 'It means that I know where I am with the menu every day and besides, he gives us big tips at Christmas.'

Charles Straven didn't pay at the end of his lunch, which he finished with China tea. Instead, the account was rendered on a monthly basis to his office and always settled promptly. He calculated that he had been lunching in the Grand for twenty two years, since he had become senior partner on the death of his father. At two o' clock he returned to his antique desk, where his assistant had laid out for him a report on the investment possibilities of the new music. He pointed out: 'singers such as Elvis Presley are generating millions of pounds of revenue for the record industry and this is expected to increase dramatically over the decade with the arrival of new entertainers who will capture the attention – and the spending power – of the young generation.'

That afternoon Charles Straven invested thirty thousand of his own money in music he would never listen to. That evening, dining on fish simmered in milk in his architecturally important Kilmacolm home with his wife, he thought about the new waitress in the Grand Hotel. He was trying to imagine her out of her uniform, in a dress, and concluded that she had attractive features and a pleasing figure. Were these the wistful thoughts of a man who had no children of his own, or a man who desired his new waitress?

On the Monday, Straven was back in his usual chair in the Grand Hotel dining-room, eating the usual fare and drinking the same brand of mineral water. But he wasn't served by the same waitress. The head waitress had decreed that his newest member of staff deserved a day off because of how quickly she had picked up the skills of waitressing, and as the stockbroker was breaking the crust of his aromatic steak pie with his silver knife, Ealasaid was wandering about the city, lingering at shop windows to study the fashions, and wondering if they would suit her. She was finding that it wasn't necessary to spend money in order to get enjoyment from shopping and when she went into Fraser Sons in Buchanan Street, she watched an elegant young woman spraying perfume from a bottle on to the back of her hand at a counter. The customer raised her hand to her nostrils, but decided that the scent didn't suit her. Ealasaid moved to her place at the counter. She had never worn perfume in her life, though at the sink of the Hebridean Hotel, with her blouse sticking to her armpits, the waitresses who stopped beside her to unload yet more dirty dishes thought that she would benefit from some deodorant and, at the end of the season, when they bought presents for each other out of the shared-out tips, they gave Ealasaid a fragrant stick.

The bottle on the counter of the Glasgow store said Sample, and Ealasaid picked it up shyly, directed the aperture on the gold button to the back of her hand and pressed. She sniffed the haze and thought she had never smelt anything so appealing in her life – not even the dog roses she stopped to sample on her way to the airless scullery of the Hebridean Hotel on a summer morning.

'Do you like it?' the immaculately made-up assistant with the black curving lashes asked.

'It's very nice,' Ealasaid conceded.

'It's a special offer, only eight pounds. And you get a free cosmetics bag with it.'

Ealasaid laid down the bottle as if it were a grenade she had been holding. That was more that she earned in a week in the Grand Hotel and though she still had savings in the bank from her labours in the Hebridean Hotel, it seemed a sin to spend that amount of money on something that, unlike the water in the sink of the island hotel, would evaporate on her skin.

Besides, she had to send money home to her parents.

That day Ealasaid ascended fearfully on her first escalator, pitching forward at the top into a small woman who gave her a murderous look. When she touched the circular rail of dresses one of them fell off and had to be restored by an assistant, leaving Ealasaid very nervous. She fled from the store and hurried up the street to the haven of the YWCA, where she lay on her side on her bed, beginning to feel homesick, not only for her parents, but for that stone sink she seemed to have been chained to, day in, day out. Shouldn't she get the evening train out of the city and stay the night in the seaport, before boarding the steamer for the island the following day?

She was lifting down her suitcase from the wardrobe when the member of staff who had befriended her and arranged her job in the Grand Hotel came in.

'Where are you going?' she asked in surprise.

'I've decided to go home.'

'But why?' Mabel asked in surprise. 'Did something happen in the Grand?'

'No. I had the day off.'

Ealasaid was persuaded to unpack her case and that evening, Mabel took her out for her first curry, a fiery dish in the Taj Mahal restaurant in Park Road that left her with a nightmare in which she had fallen into the stone sink of the Hebridean Hotel and was drowning among the obnoxious suds in the hot water. Mabel signed her up for an evening course in comptometer operating. She liked the feel and click of the keys and was complimented by the tutor on the impressive speed which she was achieving as a novice. During the day, she continued to work in the Grand Hotel and to serve Charles Straven his lunch. By this time she was looking after a dozen tables with ease and being left tips.

'How are you enjoying living and working in Glasgow?' he enquired.

'I like it very much.'

'Where do you live?'

'In the YWCA.'

'And is it comfortable?' he persisted.

'It's very nice.'

'Is the food good?'

'We're very well fed. And we have prayers every night.'

The stockbroker frowned at this item of information. When he had lost his mother as a teenager, he had become a confirmed atheist. As far as he was concerned, the life he was leading was the only one, but he hoped that he wasn't too self-indulgent or complacent. A small proportion of his income went to favoured charities, particularly cancer, since that was the disease his mother had died of. As he ate his apple charlotte, the image of his waitress down on her shapely knees in prayer, titillated him, so that he spilt a little custard on the trousers of his striped business suit.

Straven's investment in the new music was doing very well, his assistant was pleased to report. But the satisfaction of adding to his fortune no longer interested him. He had more than enough money to live in comfort for the rest of his life, on gilt-edged securities. As he sat at his desk he wasn't making calculations about new investment opportunities, but was thinking about his waitress. He had a proposition to put to her, but first he had to clear it with his wife. He raised it over dinner that night, as they were eating the fruits from the hot-house.

'I wonder if we're not asking Jessie to do too much,' he asked, referring to their housekeeper.

'What do you mean?' Gladys asked sharply, attending to her full plate.

'Well, she's getting on, so perhaps we should lighten her duties.'

'Are you suggesting that I take over some of them?' he was challenged.

'Of course not. Perhaps we should get a tablemaid, who would help with the washing up and other household chores. One of the people in the office knows this young woman who's looking for a job – '

His wife held up a hand.

'Jessie is not overburdened, I assure you. Brigid comes in two mornings a week to do the cleaning and as for the cooking, you're out for lunch except at the weekends, and I only have a bowl of soup and a banana. I don't need – or want – any other staff around me.'

Her disappointed husband knew that the matter was closed, because he had married a firebrand and he was essentially a peace-loving person who liked to retire to his study after dinner and to work at his stamp collection, one of the most notable in the country, especially strong on Penny Blacks.

The following week his waitress in the Grand had news for him.

'I'm leaving, sir.'

Charles Straven started to cough, as if some of the flaky pastry had lodged in his throat.

'Where are you going?'

'To work in an office.'

'What kind of work?'

'To operate a comptometer machine.'

'When did you acquire this skill?' he continued, intrigued.

'I've been going to night classes. I got a certificate and then I saw this job in the evening paper.'

'How much are they going to pay you?'

'Fifteen pounds a week, sir.'

'We can do better than that. Come to work for me and I'll pay you eighteen pounds a week.'

'What kind of work would that be, sir?' Ealasaid enquired, flustered.

'Working in my stockbroking office, operating a comptometer. There are a lot of calculations to be made when you're trading in stocks and shares.'

'That's very kind of you, sir.'

'Not at all. You're obviously a bright young woman. Write to the firm and tell them that you've decided not to take up their offer of a job. You'd better work here until the end of the month, to give the hotel a chance to replace you.'

Ealasaid wrote the letter of rejection to the firm that evening in her room in the YWCA and was sealing it with her tongue when Mabel came in. She told her about being offered a job by the Grand Hotel diner and the salary that went with it.

'He offered you eighteen pounds a week?' her friend said incredulously. 'What else does he want out of you?'

'I don't understand what you mean.'

'What age is this generous employer?'

'He's elderly.'

'And you say he's a stockbroker.'

'He told me that he needed a comptometer operator in his office because of the number of transactions they do in a day.'

'You're a very fortunate young woman, Ealasaid. But elderly men can be lecherous, so keep an eye on him.'

'I don't think he's that type,' Ealasaid said earnestly, adding, as if it were a character reference: 'he's been lunching every day at the Grand Hotel for years and he's very generous to the staff at Christmas.'

She didn't tell her friend that the stockbroker had started leaving a pound note for her under his pudding plate. She put it into the communal box, though it was obviously for herself. She was sending a few pounds weekly home to her parents and with the promised salary of eighteen pounds, could send more.

She served out her notice in the hotel dining-room and a few days before she was due to leave, Charles Straven asked her if she would like to come to see the office where she would be working.

'What time do you work until?' he enquired.

'Five o' clock, until afternoon teas are finished. But some days I'm on dinner.'

'What are your hours this coming Friday?'

'I start at lunch time.'

'If you come to the office at ten, I'll show you around,' he instructed her, passing her a card with the address from his wallet.

When he told his assistant that he had hired a young woman as a comptometer operator for the office, the assistant was taken aback.

'But we don't use such a machine, sir,' he pointed out.

'We'll install one. It'll speed up calculations. Arrange it with the office manager.'

The office manager was angry that the senior partner was now personally hiring staff, when he always interviewed them.

'What do we know about her?' he asked his employer.

'I know that she's an intelligent young woman who's been trained as a comptometer operator and who will be an asset in the office. I've agreed a salary of eighteen pounds a week.'

'That's surely excessive.'

'I want to reward initiative, MacFadyen. This firm was started by my grandfather who was a clerk in a counting house . . . which reminds me, I've been meaning to review your salary. I'm going to give you an increase of twenty pounds a month for your excellent work.'

The office manager went away, delighted. On the day before Ealasaid was due to go to her new employer's office Mabel went shopping with her for suitable clothes. Her friend lifted several navy and black costumes off the rails and sat outside the changing room until Ealasaid emerged.

'It's too short in the hem,' Mabel pronounced. 'You're going to work in a stockbroker's office, which will be a traditional place, so you want a smart business suit that doesn't reveal too much.'

She pronounced the next change, a high-buttoning blue outfit, with the hem below the knee, 'perfect.' Before going to bed that night Ealasaid said an earnest prayer that she would be capable of the new job. The following morning at ten she was shown into the senior partner's office by a secretary who seemed to be balanced on precarious high heels.

'I'm so glad you're joining us,' Straven said as he shook hands across his desk. He had already decided that if he showed her around himself that would only provoke gossip, so he rang for the office manager, who introduced the new arrival to the rest of the staff.

'This was bought especially for you,' he said, whipping the cover off the comptometer.

Ealasaid sat down and demonstrated her skills on the electric keyboard by using both hands to add up a list of securities, with an audience round her new swivel chair.

'That's very impressive,' the office manager complimented her.

She liked her new work, and kicked off her new and slightly uncomfortable shoes under the desk as she pressed the keys. At noon the senior partner came through to see how she was settling in.

'You seem to be doing very well,' he said, picking up a completed sheet of calculations. 'It's wonderful what can be done with machines nowadays. I'm just off to lunch at the Grand Hotel and I hope that your successor is as good at looking after me as you were.'

At lunch time, Ealasaid went out with some of the females to a café, having a bowl of soup and only joining in the conversation when she was spoken to.

'Where were you before you came to us?' she was asked by a middle-aged woman who seemed to have an excessive amount of red on her full lips.

'The Grand Hotel.'

'That's where Mr Straven goes for his lunch, isn't it?' the same questioner continued. 'How did you get in tow with him?'

Ealasaid could have objected to the choice of language, but she was a timid person who liked peace and had kept silent at the sink in the Hebridean Hotel as arguments raged behind her between the head waitress and the Italians about mistakes they had made in taking orders, giving people lobster when they had ordered beef. She explained to her made-up interrogator in the Glasgow café that she had happened to mention to Mr Straven than she had taken a course in comptometer operating at night school.

'That was very convenient,' the woman remarked and Ealasaid knew that she could be trouble in the future.

After her first day in the stockbroking office she was tired and, following supper, was thankful to step out of her new shoes and to hang her new costume in her wardrobe in the YWCA. But she was also contented as she stretched out on her bed with her Gaelic Bible. Her life in Glasgow was working out better than she could ever have hoped. She chose to read the first Book of Genesis because it was as if she had been re-born into a different world, one of possibilities and promise. However, once she had read about the miraculous energy of the seven day creation, she decided not to venture into the Garden of Eden and the consumption of the forbidden fruit by the first man and woman.

Ealasaid walked to St Columba Gaelic Church (known as the Highland Cathedral) in St Vincent Street every Sunday morning and listened intently to the sermon. She enjoyed singing the hymns and at the end of the service, a woman who had been sitting beside her in the pew approached her.

'You have a beautiful voice. Are you in a Gaelic choir?'

Ealasaid told her that she had never been in a choir in her life, apart from primary school.

'It's such a waste. You must come along for an audition with our choir.'

Ealasaid went along on the Wednesday evening to the address the woman had written down for her. The conductor took her into a side room and asked her to sing a Gaelic song.

'Which one?'

'Any one you know.'

Ealasaid knew a lot of Gaelic songs because her grandmother had lived with them and had taught her songs. She sang a plaintive song about a woman ascending a hill to watch for the boat of her lover returning from the fishing, though she feared that he had drowned in a storm.

'That was really beautiful,' the conductor enthused. 'I hope you'll join us.'

Ealasaid sang with the choir that first evening and loved the experience of the massed voices, the tenors and baritones at the back bringing a richness and depth to the evocative Gaelic songs. She went home singing quietly to herself on the bus and as she worked the keys of the calculating machine in the office, practised the repertoire of the choir in a voice that wouldn't disturb those around her.

'What's your song about?' a voice at her back requested.

She lifted her hands from the keys and swivelled round to the senior partner.

'It's a love song, sir.'

'It sounded happy.'

She could have told him that many Gaelic songs were sombre, with tragic endings, perhaps because many Gaels lived in close proximity to the unpredictable sea. Within an hour of a boat being launched on placid water, a storm could roll in from the Atlantic and swamp the craft. And there was also the threat of war, with lovers going away to enlist and not returning from the battlefields of Europe. Because her employer asked her, she gave a rough translation of the song she had been singing when he surprised her. It was about young lovers walking hand in hand across a flower-strewn meadow on a calm day on a beautiful island, with no tragedy on the horizon.

'I'm going sailing on the west coast next month,' the stockbroker disclosed. 'I hope I'll see you there.'

She looked at him with fear. Was this his way of telling her that he was dispensing with her services? Was there something wrong with the calculations she made on the machine?

'It's the Glasgow Fair, and we close the office. You'll get a fortnight's paid holiday, like the others. I presume you'll go home.'

She was thrilled at the news, and, the week before the holidays, went out to buy presents for her parents and summer clothes for herself. What would her father like? He smoked a pipe, but a supply of tobacco wasn't a very interesting present. She looked at a selection of tweed hats, including one with a feather, but decided that he wouldn't want his old cap replaced. She saw him scything in their field, the sun shimmering along the swinging blade, then stopping to light his pipe, hands cupped round the bowl to save the match from the breeze from the bay below. She decided to buy him a sleek chromium lighter, with a supply of gas, and for her mother she bought a cardigan with bone buttons.

Ealasaid had never worn trousers in her life, but she went into Richard Shops on Sauchiehall Street and tried on a blue pair with flared bottoms. As she scrutinised herself in the tilted mirror she was complimented on the fit by the assistant, particularly at the hips, so she decided to buy a white pair as well. She also bought her first pair of sneakers, blue with white laces.

On the day before the office closed for the Fair holidays the senior partner called Ealasaid along to his office, but it wasn't to talk about her work.

'When are you going home?' he quizzed her.

'Tomorrow, sir.'

'I think we can drop the sir,' he advised.

'And are you staying on the island for the whole of the fortnight?'

'Yes, Mr Straven, with my parents.'

'I would like to meet you.'

Ealasaid attributed no sinister purpose to this proposal, believing it was a paternalistic employer taking an interest in her. He told her to write down the date of his arrival on the island and also how long his yacht would be anchored there. They arranged that they would meet at five o' clock on the old jetty on the Wednesday.

9. Weighty Matters

Mary Ann Mackinnon, the manageress of Doig the bakers in
Buchanan Street, had persuaded Mr Samuel Doig that she
was preventing a potential case of food poisoning by disposing
of unsold cakes at the close of business. She was so fat that
there was no room for herself and one of the other three
assistants to serve at the same time behind the counter, a
necessity, especially at lunchtime, since people came in for
something to eat, either at the half a dozen tables, or in a
queue at the counter. By far the most popular line was meat
pies, and a Jesuit priest came down from Garnethill at noon
promptly every Monday to buy a dozen for himself and his
brethren. Workers who were demolishing the Victorian city,
and putting up ugly office blocks came in for sustenance.

It was a tight squeeze, being at the counter with Mary
Ann. But only from the serving side had she access to the

confections she had become addicted to, particularly the cream horns. By noon they were invariably 'sold out,' as she told her customers brusquely, having sold some and consumed perhaps four in the course of the morning, followed by a pie. When she walked, her nylon-clad knees made a whispering sound, as if the bakery were haunted by an unseen presence. When she went into the kitchen to ask the cook to make breakfast or high tea for a new arrival from her home island, she would be pouring with sweat. When one of the members of staff suggested the manageress should have her heart tested, that woman was dismissed on the pretext that she had been cheeky to a customer.

A further problem was added when a commercial traveller came into the bakery and opened his case to display a new line in chocolates, 'imported from the continent. Try one,' he urged Mary Ann. When she sank her teeth into the soft centre, she knew she was hooked and ordered a dozen boxes for the shop.

But Mary Ann had a big problem when she went home to the island in July for the fortnight of the Glasgow Fair. She took half a dozen cream horns with her on the train, but had consumed them and two apple turnovers by the time she reached the seaport. She had brought two boxes of the Belgian chocolates, one for herself, the other for her parents, but she finished both boxes on the hour-long sail and threw them over the sides. The gulls, as if furious at the deception, splat on her new straw hat.

'Will you look at the size of Mary Ann?' one of the stevedores observed in wonder to his fellow worker as they watched her trying to come down the gangway.

She became wedged in the gangway, causing an irritated queue of islanders who were returning home for the Fair and who were anxious to be reunited with their relatives. One of the stevedores had to go up and undo the blockage by extracting the suitcase from between her thigh and the gangway. As he did so the catches sprang and several dozen Penguin biscuits scattered on the pier, her secret hoard for the holidays. Several local boys helped themselves to the spoils before the stevedores collected the biscuits, because there was no question of Mary Ann going down on her knees to reclaim them, otherwise, as the witty stevedore remarked in Gaelic, 'we would have needed to use the derrick on the steamer to get her up on her feet again.'

Her parents lived on a croft at the top of the town. There was no bus service, and she knew that if she climbed into the solitary taxi of the town, she wouldn't be able to get out without a great deal of heaving and hauling on the part of the driver. Both her parents were in their seventies. Because she was an only child, they were pleased to see her but shocked at the size she had become. They had both come from impoverished backgrounds where sweet items were unknown in their diets, so there was nothing in the house, except a bag of sugar, to satisfy their daughter's craving. Instead of cream horns she had to be content with the cheese called crowdie which her mother made.

When she was a teenager and a half of her current weight, Mary Ann had helped out on the croft. Now she was unable to stoop to gather up the hay that her father cut with the scythe, and if she had sat beside the docile cow on the milking stool it would have collapsed underneath her. Her craving for sweet things was such that every day she waddled down the brae to the shops, where she bought up Bounty bars and Five Boys chocolate and anything else that took her fancy. She knew that her mother wouldn't approve, so she hid the hoard on the top of the wall in the byre, but unfortunately a rat with an equally sweet tooth discovered it.

At night she sat by the peat fire in the grate, telling her parents about Glasgow. Her father had never been there, but his uncle had passed through on his return from the Boer War and had reported in wonder tenements that looked like cliffs, with people living on the lighted edges. When she tried to describe a trolley bus to her intrigued father, she ran out of Gaelic. Her mother asked her about her duties in the bakers and what was sold, but when she began to describe the cream horns and the fairy cakes, her mouth began to water so much that she felt she was going to faint.

'She's an awful size,' the crofter whispered fearfully to his spouse of half a century in their bed with its brass posts under the sloping roof.

'And getting bigger by the day,' she replied. 'I made a loaf on Tuesday and she had most of it eaten by that night.'

'We had a cow like that when I was a boy,' the crofter recalled. 'It couldn't stop eating grass and it swelled and swelled so that it couldn't get up off the ground. We sent for the vet – and mark you, they were expensive even then – and he said it was colic and he stuck a blade into its stomach and it all came rushing out.'

'I don't think it's wind that Mary Ann has,' her mother said sadly. 'It's fat. I'm sorry to say this, Uilleam, but our daughter's like a pig.'

At the end of the fortnight, Mary Ann took leave of her parents and the stevedore carried her case up the gangway for her in the event of another jam. As she waited in the station, she went to the bookstall and bought an assortment of bars and bags of sweets for the train. She sat eating her way through them, wrappers scattered round her swollen ankles as the train passed some of the most magnificent scenery in Scotland.

As soon as she resumed her managerial duties on the Monday morning in Doig's, Mary Ann had the whole tray of cream horns consumed by eleven o' clock, and an hour and a half later, when the Jesuit came in for his meat pies, there wasn't an Empire biscuit left. The fortnight on the island seemed to cause a frenzy of consumption. That afternoon she broached a box of Belgian chocolates and it was empty an hour later, without the staff having been offered one. At four o' clock, when she was reaching for an apple turnover, Mary Ann collapsed behind the counter.

A doctor was phoned for. He in turn requested an ambulance, but when the stretcher was brought in, it was found that the casualty was wedged so firmly behind the counter that the combined efforts of the three shop staff, the doctor and the two ambulance men couldn't move her even an inch.

'It's like the case we had recently at Bellahouston Park,' one of the ambulance men recalled. 'A boy who was fooling about got his head stuck between two railings and the firemen had to saw away a section of the fencing which we had to take with us to the infirmary in the ambulance.'

'What are you suggesting?' the doctor asked apprehensively.

'The counter will have to be moved to get her out of here,' the ambulance man estimated.

'But it's bolted to the floor,' his mate observed.

'I'll call the fire brigade,' the doctor said wearily.

By this time a queue had gathered outside the bakery, not because they were concerned about the manageress lying prone behind the counter, but because they were wanting to buy cakes and buns. They had to be cleared away before the firemen could get in with a large monkey wrench. The staff had cleared the counter of the cakes which Mary Ann hadn't consumed and it was unbolted and lifted away.

The manageress left the bakery on a stretcher.

That evening Mary Ann came to in the women's ward.

'I'm starving!' she called out pathetically to a passing nurse.

'You're not to get anything to eat, dear – doctor's orders!' the nurse called back cheerfully as she went to empty a bedpan.

Mary Ann thought of the tray of cream horns, the boxes of Belgian chocolates and began to cry.

The following morning the consultant brought a group of medical students to the bakery manageress's bedside.

'What do you think is wrong with her?' he asked.

'Not anorexia, that's for sure,' one of the male students muttered.

'If you're so knowledgeable, Mr Sturrock, what is it?' the consultant challenged the speaker.

As he was speaking, Mary Ann was gulping a glass of water, then holding out the glass to the nurse to be refilled.

'How many has she drunk?' Sturrock asked the nurse.

'This is her sixth.'

Mary Ann was clawing at herself, but when the student lifted down the bed clothes there was no sign of a skin irritation.

'I think this patient has diabetes,' he told the consultant in a discreet voice when he rejoined the group at the foot of Mary Ann's bed.

'Quite correct, Mr Sturrock. Caused by, Mr Maclean?'

Murdo was trying to remember his text book.

'A disturbance of the normal insulin mechanism.'

'Which organ is likely to be implicated, Mr Maclean?'

'The pancreas.'

'Please elaborate, Mr Maclean.'

'The relationship of the pancreas to diabetes isn't yet fully understood, but it is known that insulin is elaborated by the beta cells of the islands of Langerhans in the pancreas. Diabetes in man may occur in association with a variety of diseases of the pancreas.'

'Good, Mr Maclean. What are some of the clinical manifestations, Miss Hutchison?' the consultant addressed an attractive female student.

'Polyuria. Patients frequently pass large amounts of urine day and night. The volume is often in excess of three or four litres. And there can be polydipsia, inordinate thirst.'

'Which, as Mr Sturrock observed, this patient is displaying,' the consultant informed the students. 'An excellent answer, Miss Hutchison. Mr Watt, what is the characteristic feature of the urine in diabetes?'

But Watt's mind suddenly went blank, or he hadn't read the chapter on Disorders of Carbohydrate Metabolism.

'Help him, Mr Neil.'

'The presence of glucose,' the studious young man answered. 'It can vary from minute traces to as much as ten per cent.'

'So what is the treatment, Miss Hooper?'

'In obese patients who are more than 50 years old, with relatively mild diabetes, the omission of free sugar from the diet – cakes, ice cream made with sugar, etcetera.'

'And in more severe cases, Miss Lamont?'

The bespectacled girl, who was known to study during every available hour, had the answer ready. 'The patient may require insulin injections.'

From her bed Mary Ann couldn't hear the conversation between the consultant and his students, but from the expression on their faces she became alarmed, since she hadn't yet been given the diagnosis. When her blood had been analysed in the lab the technician had called out: 'There's more sugar than blood here!' Mary Ann began to imagine that she had cancer and that they were reluctant to tell her. That was when she began to cry and her howls brought two nurses to her bedside.

'There are people sleeping in this ward!' they warned her.

'I'm going to die!' she wailed.

'Nonsense. The consultant will be round later to chat to you.'

'Can I have a cup of tea and a biscuit?' she requested hopefully.

'Not on your life – you could go into a coma.'

That answer set her wailing again and the consultant had to be sent for. He sat by her bed and explained that she had diabetes and would require to lay off sweet things and to inject herself.

'But I hate the sight of needles!'

'I'm afraid there's no other way,' the consultant informed her abruptly.

Meantime Murdo Maclean was divesting himself of his white coat and preparing to go back to Maclay Hall for his strictly rationed supper. But a thought was nagging at him. In the bloated features of the female patient with Type 2 diabetes he was sure that he recognised a familiar face and on the way out of the Infirmary he made a detour of the ward and unhooked the board from the end of the bed.

'I thought it was you, Mary Ann.'

She looked at him, bewildered.

'I'm Murdo Maclean, the bank manager's son,' he said, extending a hand.

'Of course you are. I remember when you were a toddler on reins on Main Street, and your mother had a job keeping you on the pavement. So you're a doctor.'

'Not yet,' he cautioned. 'How are you?'

'I've just had terrible news. I've got diabetes and I'll have to inject myself for the rest of my life. I can't bear the thought of it,' she began to sob.

'You'll soon get used to it,' he reassured her.

'And I've not to eat any more sweet things.'

'That'll make a difference to your health. You'll feel so much better.'

'But I work in a baker's shop,' she explained, as if that excused her corpulence.

Murdo told her that he would come and see her again,

and that night on the phone to the island he reported to his mother than Mary Ann was in the infirmary.

'I'm not surprised. I saw her when she was home for the summer, and she could hardly get along Main Street. I said to your father: "that woman's going to be in a wheelchair soon, and who's going to push her up and down the brae?" Are you attending to your studies and not spending too much time on that accordion?'

Two days later Murdo went to visit Mary Ann again, but found her bed occupied by another patient.

'She's gone home,' a nurse explained. 'We gave her a lesson on how to inject herself and a supply of insulin. She went away quite the thing.'

Mary Ann dreaded returning to Doig's and being confronted by the trays of cream horns and Empire biscuits which she had consumed so gluttonously. But as she reached out for a confection she heard the voice of the consultant warning her: 'if you ignore our advice you could end up having an infected toe that would have to be removed and then we might have to consider removing the foot, and so on.'

The girls in the shop made a big fuss of her and they found that as she began to shed weight, they could easily pass her behind the counter. At the end of the month she had lost two stones and in her room and kitchen on New City Road, as she studied her face in the mirror, she began to see signs of prettiness as her nose began to emerge from the mass. Before she had washed her own hair and cut it with scissors, but for the first time she went to Defazio's salon in St George's Road.

'What kind of cut would you like, madam?' the assistant

with the incredibly small waist and long eyelashes asked.

'What would suit?'

There were photographs of Sandie Shaw and Lulu on the wall and Mary Ann decided to go for the Lulu look. As she was going back to the shop, a workman whistled at her from a high ladder. When she went into Doig's they didn't recognise her at first and they shrieked that she looked 'fabulous!'

A week later Mr Doig walked into his own shop.

'I wish to see the manageress,' he asked Mary Ann.

'I am the manageress.'

'I didn't recognise you,' he blinked behind his potent spectacles. 'Can you explain why the takings have suddenly gone up by ten per cent?'

At school they had told Mary Ann that she was gifted enough at maths to go on and read that subject at university. But she had also the innate cunning of the islander when confronted with an awkward situation.

'You remember I told you that I had to dispose of unsold confections at the close of business in case of food poisoning, especially in cream-based products, Mr Doig? I recall telling you about a food poisoning outbreak in Rutherglen where the bakery was shut down by health officials.'

'What has that got to do with an increase in takings?' he challenged her.

'I found a way of stopping the wastage at the close of business. I tell my regulars: if you come in after three o' clock you'll be entitled to a ten per cent discount on any perishable item that you buy. Isn't that better than throwing good cakes into the swill bin to feed pigs, Mr Doig?'

He beamed at his manageress's business acumen.

'I'd like you to come to head office, to be my personal assistant and help me expand my business, Miss Mackinnon.'

'I'm honoured, Mr Doig, but I prefer direct contact with my customers, and will remain here, serving them – and you – if you don't mind, Mr Doig.'

'I'm putting two pounds a week on to your wages,' he told her before leaving the most profitable shop in his chain.

However, Mary Ann continued to dispense free meals to islanders arriving off the train in the unfamiliar city. And she also continued her weekly visit to Mrs MacCaig's house in Ashley Street.

'My God, you're a different person,' Mrs MacCaig enthused.

'I've lost five stone and I'm going to lose as much again,' the bakery manageress said proudly as she poured drams from the half bottle she had bought. 'I was buying my clothes at Evans Outsizes on Sauchiehall Street, but now I can go into any shop.'

As they toasted her continuing reduction, Seamus the young policeman came in from his shift. He didn't recognise Mary Ann from the rear and when she turned round he was startled by her attractiveness. A very shapely nose and expressive eyes had emerged from the bloated face and the hounds' dewlaps had disappeared, revealing a shapely neck. At that moment he fell in love with her. The following week they were dancing a Canadian Barn dance in the Highlanders' Institute, an activity which Mary Ann could never have survived in her previous immobility. Now she found herself hopping round the floor without breaking sweat and at the end the policeman hugged her and bought her a lemon drink.

10. Artistic Licence

Iain MacGilp had gone to school with Murdo Maclean in
the same mainland town. MacGilp's mother was a gentle
widow, her husband having been a Swordfish pilot shot down
in the battle over Malta. There was some money on the
mother's side of the family and she indulged her only child,
probably because he had the same dark good looks as her
husband. He dressed very elegantly and had his swept-back
hair cut regularly by an Italian barber. He was clever but lazy,
and school was an effortless imposition. He was probably the
first person in the town to have acquired a copy of *Waiting
for Godot* and after school, in a café at the top of Edward
Street, he tried to explain existentialism to Murdo Maclean.
MacGilp smoked a thin intellectual pipe, tamping the glowing
mass down with the end of a knife as he discoursed.

He was the most accomplished dancer in the school,

having attended ceilidhs since the age of fifteen and having natural grace and co-ordination. At the senior school dance there was a race across the floor towards him for the Ladies' Choice as the other males sat on the benches as if their spines had been nailed to the wall. He and Murdo decided that they would both apply for Maclay Hall, but they didn't get to share a room, which was just as well with regard to Murdo's studies, because Iain had apparently come to university to have a good time. In the summer before matriculating he had worked in a bookmakers in his native town because he was good at mental arithmetic and could calculate betting slips. His pay (supplemented by astute bets) allowed him to buy a Triumph motor cycle and he applied himself to passing his driving test with a dedication which he would never accord to his studies. He received his licence a week before going to Glasgow. He drove himself there, his suitcase strapped precariously to the pillion. On Loch Lomond-side he was stopped for speeding, but because the traffic policeman was from the same town, Iain was cautioned, not charged.

The Triumph was black and the new owner kept the chromework gleaming. When he should have been up at Gilmorehill, listening to a lecture on Kant's Critique, he was in Maclay Hall's garage, servicing his machine in a boiler suit. He didn't dare take the bike to the city's dance halls he frequented because it would be stolen and probably shipped to Ireland, where, with new number plates, it would roar along a single-track road in Donegal.

Having danced in either the Highlanders' Institute or the Locarno on the Friday evening, he would speed out of the city on the Saturday. His destination was Helensburgh. In his first week at university he had gone dancing in the Majestic Ballroom in Hope Street and had asked a young woman up for a quickstep.

'You dance beautifully,' this very attractive woman complimented him as he steered her round the floor. She introduced herself as Evelyn and her blonde hair fell beyond her shoulders. 'What do you do?'

'Apart from dancing? I'm a student.'

'Of what?'

'Philosophy.'

'You must have a good mind as well as good footwork.'

'It doesn't follow,' her partner cautioned her as he turned her at the appropriate time in the racy music. 'Philosophy is what you want it to be.'

'Should I know who said that?' Evelyn asked, impressed.

'I did. What do you do?'

'I'm an artist.'

'A painter? Oils or watercolours?'

'The new medium, acrylic.'

'Isn't that what people put on the woodwork of their houses?' he asked as the music stopped and he was leading her back to her seat.

'I put it on boards because canvas is too expensive.'

They sat out the foxtrot so that they could exchange information about each others' lives.

'I was married, but my husband preferred someone else even after the nuptials. No, that's not quite accurate. I must remember that I'm talking to a philosopher. He was having a relationship before we were married and he carried it on thereafter. I caught them in bed – our bed,' she added factually.

'I presume you're single.'

'On what basis do you make that deduction?' he challenged her as he lit his pipe.

'Because you're here alone and you're a student. Where do you stay?'

'In a university hall called Maclay.'

'And is it comfortable?'

'I hardly notice. I only use it to sleep in.'

'Where do you do your studies, then?' she asked, intrigued and attracted by this well-groomed young man with the pipe between his perfect teeth. She wondered if he had Italian blood.

'I don't do much studying because I find the course boring.'

'But you pass your exams?'

'I haven't sat any yet. Where do you live?'

'Overlooking the Holy Loch. Do you know that area?'

'It's near Dunoon, isn't it?'

'Yes. You must come and visit me.'

A cha-cha was called and they rose to dance. At the end of the evening they arranged that Iain would visit the following Saturday.

Instead of studying one of the set texts in philosophy, Iain MacGilp pored over a map, deciding the route he would take on his motor bike on the Saturday. He was at the Highlanders' Institute on the Friday, dancing waltzes and reels with his usual composed elegance, and after breakfast in Maclay the next morning, he set out. He followed the tortuous road along Loch Lomond, taking care on this trip not to fall foul of a police patrol. At Tarbet he cut through and throttled up the Rest and Be Thankful, descending at ninety miles an hour to Loch Fyne and roaring along beside its quiet waters until he reached his destination.

Evelyn had lunch ready for him, with a bottle of wine. They sat in the conservatory of her charming cottage overlooking the Holy Loch.

'It's a wonderful view,' he enthused as he ate fresh fish.

'But spoiled by that monstrosity down there.'

Evelyn was referring to the large grey vessel anchored below which had arrived the previous year to much opposition, the depot ship of the base for US Navy submarines, armed with nuclear deterrents against the Russian threat. But Iain MacGilp hadn't participated in the heated discussions in Maclay Hall about Scotland being targeted by Soviet weapons of mass destruction because of the American presence on the loch in Argyll. When the common room was full of outraged voices he was either on the dance floor, or lying beside his motor bike in the garage, vital parts spread out around him. His greatest pride was not in understanding David Hume, but in being able to strip down and reassemble a gear box.

After fresh fruit from her own garden Evelyn took him into her studio to show him her paintings. The one in progress on the easel was of the view from the conservatory window, but with the depot ship left out. Iain lit his pipe while contemplating it, as if he were an art critic.

'Do you like it?'

'I do,' he told her sincerely.

'It's a commission from a lady on this side of the loch. She's in her seventies and she told me that she's likely to go before the Americans leave. She wanted a painting to remind her of how the loch used to be.'

'That's fair enough,' he conceded.

'I also paint people,' she informed him. 'I teach part-time up at the Art School in Glasgow and I keep a studio in Kent Road. That's where my sitters come.' She turned round a painting that was leaning against a wall. 'This is waiting to go to the framers. You won't recognise him, but he owns one of the biggest shipyards on the Clyde and has an estate near Dunoon. He asked me to paint him for his board room. I'm honoured, because this is going to be hung beside the portrait of his father done by Sargent.'

Her guest studied the head and shoulders of the smug looking man, a gold chain crossing his waistcoat.

'It allows me to keep this cottage,' Evelyn said, as if apologising.

'Good.'

'Is that a philosophical observation?'

Half an hour later they were lying in her bed, sharing a cigarette, his arm behind his sleek head.

'When are we going dancing again?' she asked.

'Whenever you want.'

'Is it only ballroom that you do?'

'I go to the Highlanders for ceilidh, and to the Barrowland.'

'You go to the Barrowland?' she asked in surprise. 'Isn't that a den of iniquity?'

'Who told you that?' he asked with his usual cool manner which some people found boorish. But he was a man of few words. When you had a woman in your arms on the dance floor, it wasn't necessary to converse.

'I heard it's a rough place.'

'Rough is the wrong word,' he corrected her, as if considering a proposition in philosophy. 'It's a vibrant place. Have you heard of the Twist?'

'I haven't. It sounds like an injury you do to your back.'

'It's the latest dance. Have you heard of Chubby Checker?'

'The name doesn't mean a thing to me. Is he an artist?'

'Not your kind of artist. He's an American singer with a hit called "Let's Twist Again."'

'What kind of dance is it?' Evelyn asked, intrigued.

'It's been described as one where you try to stub out a cigarette with your toe while drying your back with a towel,' the philosophy student informed her.

'It sounds interesting. When can we try it?'

'Next weekend?'

'Sounds fun.'

'The thing is, you wouldn't want to wear the same dress that you wore last week to the Majestic,' he cautioned her.

'Why not?'

'Because it's a different style of dancing. The females at Barrowland usually wear quite short dresses when they're doing the Twist.'

'What are you trying to get me to show, Iain?'

But on the Monday she descended from the Art School on to Sauchiehall Street and went into Richard Shops, one of the first boutiques in Glasgow, and tried on several dresses before choosing one whose hem ended at the knee, having decided that modesty was important. On the Friday she met Iain and they took a taxi to the Barrowland. Evelyn was enchanted by the spectacle of hundreds of dancers jiving to the swinging music of Billy Macgregor and the Gaylords, the women with their short hems riding up round their thighs, the men in smart suits and swept-back hair styles plastered down with brilliantine. Evelyn and her escort found a space on the floor and soon she was uninhibitedly in the swing of the music. In front of her, Iain's shining shoes went in and out as she squirmed down.

'That was fabulous,' she told him as they drank lemonade on a sofa in a quiet corner. 'How often do you come here?'

'When I feel like it.'

'How many dance halls do you actually go to?' she interrogated him.

'I go to most of them,' he disclosed as he reamed his pipe.

'How many of them are there?'

'Maybe about fifteen. I don't know, I've never counted them.'

'Which are your favourites?' she persisted.

'I like the Plaza and the Albert. They're very formal places. But I like coming here, because it's much freer. And as I told you, I also go to the Highlanders' Institute for ceilidh dancing.'

'Won't they put you out if you spend so much time dancing and don't pass your exams?'

'That's a proposition I haven't considered yet. Let's dance again.'

That night he drove her home to the Holy Loch on his motor bike. She clasped his waist, her hair streaming in the breeze under the stars rushing past overhead. She trusted this man who seemed to handle his machine so expertly on the bends, though at one place she felt heather raking her bare leg. He had become so involved with her that he was spending half the week with her, though he was still paying for his room in Maclay Hall. He didn't bring his philosophy textbooks with him in the panniers when he went down to the Holy Loch, but read translations of the novels of Camus and Sartre.

Iain MacGilp was probably the first existentialist to have emerged from the Scottish Highlands. On the days when Evelyn was in Glasgow, teaching at the Art School, he went walking in the hills and had the log fire blazing and a meal ready when she returned in the evening. They continued to patronise the ballrooms of Glasgow at the weekends and when he took her to the Highlanders' Institute and spun her in Strip the Willow, she seemed to be floating down the set. If they danced until late, they didn't return to the Holy Loch, but instead bedded down on the folding-down sofa in her studio, beside the table of squeezed-out tubes, the uncompleted portrait of an industrial baron watching them from the easel.

'I'd like to paint you,' she told him one evening as he was drying the supper dishes in the little kitchen off the studio in Kent Road.

'I can't afford your fee.'

'This isn't about commerce, it's about love. I'll paint you at home, instead of here.'

She arranged him sitting in an antique chair in the conservatory, with the backdrop of the loch. He had his pipe in his mouth and his expression was contemplative. As she painted in her smock, they discussed their next dancing venue.

'It becomes an addiction, doesn't it?' she queried as she worked on the dark stem of the pipe.

'It does, but a pleasant addiction.'

'So could you give it up?'

'I would find it very difficult.'

'You could become a dance teacher.'

'I prefer to be on the floor using my own feet, not telling others where to put theirs.'

She draped a cloth over the painting after each session because she didn't want him to see it until it was finished. On the afternoon she applied the last strokes, she cooked a special supper of seafood and opened a bottle of quality champagne before she unveiled her work.

At first she thought his silence as he studied it meant that he didn't approve.

'I like it very much.'

'I would give it to you to hang in your room in Maclay, but I can't bear to part with it. When you're not here I have it to look at.'

They had been dancing in the Barrowland but instead of staying in the studio in the city they decided to drive back to the cottage. The wind was lifting her short dress as they sped along the quiet country roads, an owl flapping across in the headlamp.

'I could have sworn I locked the door,' she said, when she turned the handle.

There was someone sitting in the conservatory. She gripped Iain's arm as the silhouette spoke.

'I was expecting you to be here to welcome me home.'

When she snapped on the light, a man in an American sailor's uniform was sitting in the wicker chair, his cap on the glass table.

'When did you come back?' she asked truculently.

'Yesterday. They decided to post me back to the depot ship. You don't sound happy to see me. Introduce me to your friend.'

'This is Iain MacGilp.'

The big man rose audibly from the wicker chair and gripped the philosophy student's hand.

'Glad to meet you, Iain MacGilp. Maybe you can explain what you're doing out so late with my wife.'

Since his schooldays, Iain MacGilp had been renowned for his composure. He had sat impassively while he was berated for not handing in homework, and on the floor of the Barrowland had expertly steered his partner past the sinister looking Teddy boy, the hem of his jacket brushing the floor as he Twisted. But tonight his voice faltered.

'Your wife?' He turned to his lover. 'I thought you were divorced.'

'Oh no,' the cuckolded husband said. 'Tell him how long we've been married, honey.'

'Three years too long.'

'You thought you'd got rid of me when I was posted back to the States. Well, here I am back, and what do I find, someone's pyjamas under my pillow? And this.' He pointed to the portrait of his wife's lover on the easel. 'I ain't really into art, but I admit, it's a good likeness.' As he was talking he took a knife from his pocket and sprang the blade. 'But I don't like someone messing about with my wife.'

He walked across to the canvas and slashed it several times.

'You bastard! Get out of here!' Evelyn screamed.

He threw her aside and advanced towards the philosophy student with the blade. Iain MacGilp knew that he couldn't allow fear to render him immobile. He realised that the man advancing towards him would use the knife, and that he could end up in the loch below. He was looking around for something to stop the assault, but there was nothing within reach, so he moved behind the glass table. As his assailant approached Iain picked up the table and heaved it at him, then turned and ran out of the door. Evelyn was pursuing him as well as her husband as he ran down the dark path to the shed where he had left his motor cycle. He bestrode it and kick-started it. In the beam of the light he saw the American sailor coming along the path, the knife still in his hand, blood running from his hand from the impact of the glass-topped table. He ran the motor bike towards him, forcing him into the shrubbery. As he was going down the path Evelyn took a short cut to keep up with him, trying to get onto the pillion but he throttled away into the night.

11. The Twist

When Marsaili came to Glasgow to continue her education she didn't go into Doig the bakers to be welcomed to the city and fed by Mary Ann. Marsaili's brother Murdo was at Buchanan Street Station when the steam train pulled in after its long haul from the west coast. However, Marsaili could easily have held a conversation in Gaelic with the bakery manageress, since she was the only one of Archie Maclean's four children who had learned the language, to the scepticism of her siblings.

'Why are you wasting your time on a dead language?' Calum the would-be writer provoked her, a cigarette in his fingers, the scent of whisky on his breath. He had just come from listening to the latest Elvis on the Sea Breezes Café jukebox on Main Street.

But his sister didn't need to justify her decision to him.

150

She had mastered Gaelic, partly out of love and respect for her father, who was obsessed with it, but also because she wanted to know what visitors to the bank house were saying, instead of having it translated for her. She knew, of course, that she was one of very few of her generation in the small town who was learning the language, but that didn't deter her.

Brother and sister didn't take a tram from Buchanan Street since that mode of transport had been disbanded, though the rails were still embedded in certain streets. Instead Marsaili had been given money by her parents to take a taxi to her hall of residence. She had come to Glasgow University to study veterinary science, since from infancy she had been passionate about animals and, on one notorious occasion in the annals of Maclean family history, had lifted from the road a rat that had been run over. The crippled animal was still alive and had bitten her for her charity and she had had to go up to Doctor Murdoch to have a tetanus injection in her buttock. Even that humiliating experience didn't deter her from the rescue work she undertook. She had once given her brother Murdo a row for having brought home a baby owl that had fallen from a nest, instructing him that the parents might even then be looking for it.

Marsaili appreciated the fierceness of the competition to study veterinary science and understood that it was a long and rigorous course, with animals due at least as much attention as humans did in medicine. She has inherited her mother's striking features and dark manageable hair cut short to the base of the neck and the taxi driver is admiring her in the mirror above as he drives them to the new Wolfson Hall of Residence at Garscube Estate. Marsaili hoped for a study bedroom to herself, but she's having to share. Her roommate is already in residence and when Marsaili opens the door she's met by a blast of music and a young woman with a blonde ponytail swaying her hips to rock and roll played on a Dansette deck. Marsaili sets down her case and stands watching the performance to the end, noting the snapping fingers above the dancer's head, the tartan mini-skirt rotating horizontally, blue knickers showing.

'Oh hi,' the dancer says when the number ends and she is about to lift the arm and play it again. 'I'm Moira Dunsyre,' she identifies herself, holding out a hand.

'I'm Marsaili.'

Her room-mate repeats the name, like a mantra.

'I'm taking the bed nearest the door,' Moira informs her.

Marsaili nods and lifts her case on to the other bed and begins unpacking, having been shown the hanging space and drawers which are hers.

'What are you studying?' Moira asks.

'Veterinary science.'

'Four people from my school tried for it but couldn't get a place anywhere, though they had high grades.'

'And you?' Marsaili enquires.

'Music.'

'Music?' Marsaili repeats, surprised.

'Yes. It's the only thing I was good at at school. My father plays the violin.'

'Do you play an instrument?'

'The piano.'

'Then why aren't you at the College of Music?'

'I did apply, but they didn't want me, but Glasgow said yes. I'm going to study to be a music teacher, but I hope I'll never have to teach. I want to learn the guitar, form my own band and make a fortune.'

This intimation causes Marsaili some concern as she folds away in the drawer the blouses that her mother ironed so carefully for her, along with a supply of woollens because, she said, the city could be very cold. Has she been put in with a person who's going to be playing a guitar and records most of the time, in which case she'll be unable to study in this room?

But surely there are rules about playing music too loudly.

'Smoke?' her roommate asked, offering a packet of cigarettes.

Now this is even more serious than the sound from the Dansette. Marsaili's parents are both smokers and the sitting-room in the bank house seemed to have a permanent blue haze. She had hoped she was getting away from that unhealthy habit. She opens the window but Moira puts her cigarette into her mouth and hugs her shoulders to show that she's cold in her skimpy clothes, so Marsaili compromises by leaving the window open a little.

They go down to supper together and Marsaili is intrigued by the way her roommate balances the peas on her fork before raising them to her mouth. Afterwards, in the lounge, she lights up and has this habit of making her mouth into an O and blowing the smoke as if she's intent on creating rings. Before going up to bed Marsaili phones her parents to reassure them that she has arrived safely and is settling in, but she doesn't tell them that she has a roommate addicted to cigarettes and rock and roll music, because she knows that her mother's response will be to go and tell the warden that you want another room.

The Dansette isn't played again that evening and Moira doesn't have a snoring problem. But she does speak in her sleep – or rather moan. Marsaili lies listening, but she isn't sure if the female in the other bed is in pain or ecstasy. Could it be that she's having a passionate dream? At last Moira sinks into soundless sleep, but in the morning, when it's time to go down to breakfast, Marsaili has great difficulty arousing her from her comatose state, as if she's taken some pill.

Marsaili wondered why her first term's lectures for her degree in veterinary medicine and surgery should have a course on botany, until she realised that animals ate plants. The other lectures were in chemistry and physics, subjects she had studied at school, but on Wednesday morning there was a class on animal management, when the demonstrator showed the students how to handle a cat. It was going to be hard work, which is why, when she went back to Wolfson Hall in the early evening, she was annoyed to hear her roommate's Dansette. Rather than have a row with her, Marsaili decided to study in one of the quiet rooms downstairs and at supper she sat with fellow students in vet science.

At the end of her first week as a student, Marsaili visited her brother at Maclay Hall and was introduced to his friends, including Brogan, who seemed to make a special effort to be well-mannered and personable. Murdo is in his third year in medicine and has acquired a slight moustache as well as confidence. He passed the crucial test of not being squeamish when the vat was opened and he saw his first cadaver which

Maclay Days

he was expected to dissect. Two rows away there was a clatter as a female student dropped her scalpel. She had been fine when first shown a dead body, but when asked to make an incision, she fainted. She was helped to a chair by the demonstrator and the following day had an interview with the professor at which it was agreed that, if she couldn't stand broken skin and blood, that didn't mean that she wouldn't be able to function as a GP, though they were required to stitch cuts.

'Give it time, Miss Taylor,' the professor advised gently. 'We'll see how you're coping in a month's time.'

However, she transferred from medicine to biochemistry and was much happier among test tubes.

Marsaili went with her brother to the Highlanders' Institute to listen to him playing in the dance band, having already been warned that this activity was not to be relayed to their parents, since Alice wanted her elder son to concentrate on his studies. But he was playing regularly in the band and also courting the dark-haired beauty Una from Islay whom he had met at the now burnt-out St Andrew's Halls. From the moment she was introduced to Una at the Highlanders' Institute, Marsaili knew that her brother couldn't have found a better girl. Marsaili was asked up to waltz by a young man who turned out to be a third year student of Celtic Studies. His name was Roderick Mackenzie from Ross-shire. He was tall and earnest and wore a blazer with the university badge and creased grey flannels. He was a Gaelic learner who had been inspired to take the course because though his grandparents had had the language, it hadn't been passed on to his mother and therefore his father hadn't spoken it to his children.

Marsaili told him (in Gaelic) that she had been in the same position, with a non-Gaelic speaking mother, but had spoken Gaelic with her father in the face of ridicule from her siblings. She noticed how hesitant Roderick's Gaelic was as they sat out the dances with a lemonade each.

'We don't get enough spoken Gaelic in the class,' he complained. 'Plenty of grounding in grammar, but not enough conversation. I come here, not because I'm all that interested in dancing, but because I know I'll meet Gaels here and be able to have a conversation with them, to improve my spoken Gaelic.'

Marsaili thought that this was brave of him. She was attracted to his quiet personality and his commitment to the language he had been denied at birth. They danced a Strip the Willow and she was pleased how careful he was to hold her by the elbow so that he wouldn't bruise her arm, unlike those back home who threw their partners about the dance floor.

'Will I see you here next Friday?' he asked.

'That depends. I came tonight because my brother Murdo's playing in the band. That's him on second accordion.'

'They make a good sound,' Roderick said.

'Our parents don't know that he's playing in the band. He's a medical student and my mother in particular would fret that he wasn't paying enough attention to his studies. I'll go and ask him if he's playing here next week.'

She came back to inform the student of Celtic that the band was playing at a function in the Grand Hotel the following Friday, but in a fortnight's time it would be back at the Highlanders' venue. They made a date to meet then.

Maclay Days

Moira continued to pollute their sleeping quarters with her cigarettes. She had increased her consumption, collecting coupons for a hairdryer and while she was watching the lecturer showing them how to handle the domestic dog, Marsaili could smell the smoke on her sleeve and was sure that the student sitting beside her must think her a chain-smoker.

'We should have a night out together,' Moira proposed towards the end of October, when they were sitting at supper together and a bitter wind was sweeping the dark streets of Glasgow, causing Marsaili to think of all the stray animals out there, hungry, huddling for shelter. She was beginning to acknowledge to herself that she cared more for animals than for people and when anyone complained '*he or she is behaving like an animal*', Marsaili would protest and tell them that you cannot attribute wickedness to any creature.

'A night out?' the vet student asked for clarification.

'Let's go to a Halloween party. There's one in the Locarno.'

'The Locarno?'

'It's a dance hall down on Sauchiehall Street.'

'But we'll have to dress up,' Marsaili pointed out.

At home there had been fierce competition among the mothers to produce the most eye-catching costume for the Halloween party in the hall and Marsaili had won several times, with, famously, a fairy whose flimsy wings lit up, thanks to the ingenuity of the local electrician, a friend of her father's, who had concealed coloured bulbs in the wings and made a little bag for her to carry the battery under her costume.

'We don't have to have full costumes. We'll get masks and a few decorations,' Moira reassured her roommate.

On Saturday they went into the city together, to a shop in Queen Street which sold cushions that made rude noises, life-like rubber snakes and conjuring tricks. Moira bought a gold Egyptian mask and Marsaili, who was becoming less enthused by the idea of accompanying her roommate to the unknown Locarno, settled for a cat's mask, with realistic whiskers.

Moira sought out the housekeeper in the hall of residence and persuaded her (with a box of chocolates) to lend them a couple of curtains from the linen store. The one chosen by Moira was gold and she wrapped it round her body, making sure it was tight, so that with the mask she would present as a seductive Cleopatra. Marsaili chose a striped one to simulate fur.

The cat and the Egyptian queen decided that it was too risky to take a bus into the city in their costumes, so they shared a taxi. As soon as they were inside the door the music was deafening, but Marsaili was enchanted by the band on the rotating stage and by the variety of costumes on the dance floor. The latest dance craze was the Twist, but it hadn't reached the island by the time that Marsaili left, so she had to stand watching, to try to get the hang of the movements.

She was pulled on to the dance floor by a devil, in a horned mask and a trailing tail. He held her by her right hand, raised his left in the air and began to move his hips as though he were grinding cigarette butts into the polished floor with his pointed black shoes. Marsaili could hear the beat but it was difficult fitting her feet to it.

Then he stopped dancing. Had she made a wrong move? Was she a poor partner for this Twist specialist who seemed to have special muscles at the base of his spine, allowing him to rotate his hips through one hundred and eighty degrees?

Marsaili heard clapping and turned to see Moira in the centre. Despite the tight costume, the Egyptian queen was still able to Twist in a spectacular way, hips thrust from side to side, the gold shoes on her feet pounding the floor. She was clapping her hands above her head as her partner, dressed as Robert the Bruce, with a gold crown and wearing a blue silk cloak, performed opposite her.

Marsaili was enchanted, as were the other dancers, at the meeting of these two immortal figures from history. The trumpeter was trying to blow more power from his gold instrument and the saxophone dazzled as it was swung from side to side. The drummers' sticks hammered the taut skin. And when the dancers, hands joined, were bowing to the thunderous applause, they were each presented with a bottle of champagne.

'Can I see you home?' Marsaili's dancing partner, his devil's mask up on his forehead to reveal an uninteresting face, asked at her elbow.

'Thank you, but I've arranged to go home with my friend.'

Marsaili found her roommate sitting at a table with her dancing partner, his realistic wooden battleaxe lying by his hand.

'This is Sean,' Moira introduced him.

Marsaili could see the dark attraction of the Irish in his features, but his eyes looked hard, as if he resented the struggle his folks had had to survive when they fled the potato famine in their native land. She saw the small cross dangling from the heavy gold links of the chain round his wrist, but she knew that that didn't signify piety. Sinister was the word she said to herself as she studied the fake king of Scotland.

'Have you two met before?' Marsaili enquired, since they were holding hands across the table.

'We have,' he answered for the smiling queen.

That night Marsaili went back to the Hall alone.

12. Entitlement

Ealasaid MacAllister had come down to the city with her father's old suitcase, but returned with a new one, full of presents and new clothes and also with her Gaelic Bible wrapped in a pair of her new trousers. The train would be packed with city expatriates returning to their native island for the Fair, passing round bottles of whisky as they sang in Gaelic, but Ealasaid was at the station an hour before the departure and found a seat. A middle-aged man lifted her suitcase up into the rack. She sat at the window in the sun, reading a magazine.

The stevedores standing in the shade of the store, watching the homecoming islanders descending the gangway, didn't recognise the young woman who had left surreptitiously. She had her hair cut short for her holiday and she was wearing a bright dress of floral material from Coplands which blew between her legs as she set down her suitcase on the pier. She wanted to surprise her parents and hadn't written to tell them that she was coming home for a fortnight. She made several halts on the steep brae in the heat and at the top she surveyed the bay and remembered how heartbroken she had been to have left the place of her birth when she had gone aboard the steamer with her shame.

Her father was scything the hay as she approached the croft and when he saw her the blade stopped round his boots as if he had seen a ghost. He shouted to his wife and when she emerged from the house in her apron, she stood looking at her daughter as though she were a stranger.

'Why did you leave us with a letter but without a word?' she asked Ealasaid in Gaelic. 'We were worried to death and your father didn't sleep for weeks.'

'I wrote to you from Glasgow.'

'Yes, but there was no real explanation as to why you left in the first place.'

Ealasaid knew that she had to provide one before she would be allowed back in her home. The fierce sun was on her bare arms as she explained that she had become weary of washing dishes and scouring pots in the Hebridean Hotel, and wanted to try to make a life for herself.

'You could have got another job here,' her father persisted.

'I know it was wrong of me and I prayed every night for guidance.'

That confession seemed to assuage her parents and she passed under the lintel and up the steep narrow stairs to her room, which was exactly as she had left it on the morning she had gone on the steamer. After she had made her bed, she helped her mother to prepare the supper of potatoes from their own ground and the pail of fish that a neighbour with a boat had handed in. Ealasaid had always enjoyed mackerel, but this evening she found them coarse, her palate having been changed by the varied meals in the YWCA.

After supper she gave her parents their presents. Her mother was appreciative of the cardigan and kept smoothing down its wool. She had to show her father how to use the lighter and how the flame could be made taller by turning the little serrated wheel. She saw how awkwardly he handled it before he laid it on the table. He read from the Gaelic Bible, as he had done each evening since he was a young man. When Ealasaid had settled in her hard narrow bed under the coombed ceiling and had said her prayers, she felt depressed and guilty at her lack of joy at being home. She would never have imagined that she would have missed the bustle of the city, the roar of the traffic, the clatter of typewriters in the office. The next day she put on old clothes and went out to help her father, raking up the hay and carrying its prickly fragrance in armfuls to form a stack. She noticed that her father was lighting his pipe with his usual box of matches instead of with her gas-fired gift.

On her second evening at home Ealasaid went for a walk around the top of the town, cutting down past the tennis courts of the Hebridean Hotel. She saw Bella the head waitress having a smoke at the bottom of the steps at the back door, beside the dustbins.

'I wouldn't have known you unless you had spoken,' Bella told her. 'You're not the same lassie that was up to her elbows in that sink. What are you doing with yourself?'

Ealasaid told her that she was operating a comptometer in a stockbrokers' office in Glasgow.

'I always felt that there was more to you,' the head waitress observed. 'The deep ones are the ones who don't say anything and get on with their work. No matter the pile of dishes beside you, you never complained. The girl we have doing your job now is very slow and clumsy and more dishes end up in pieces on the floor at her feet than back in the cupboard. We have Carlo back with us this summer.'

Ealasaid received this information in silence and without enthusiasm. She had no time for the Italian who had seduced her with sparkling wine from a stolen bottle. On the Wednesday she put on her new blue trousers and sneakers and was sitting on the wall of the old pier by four thirty, waiting to meet her employer.

Charles Straven kept his forty-five feet schooner on the Clyde and brought it through the Crinan Canal to the west every July, using a crew of Glasgow University students. They swarmed about the deck as he stood by the tiller in his white-topped yachting cap, bringing the boat into the bay. When it was moored safely he allowed the crew to go ashore in the larger of the rubber roundabouts and he rowed himself across to the old pier in the smaller one. He embraced Ealasaid and invited her on board.

'You were brought up in a beautiful place,' he remarked as he rowed her skilfully with powerful strokes among the anchored craft. 'I'm surprised that you would want to leave it for a place like Glasgow.'

But she couldn't tell him that she had left because she thought she was pregnant by an Italian waiter.

He helped her up on to the teak deck and gave her a conducted tour of the spacious yacht that had been built for a Glasgow shipowner in his own yard in the extravagant 1920s. He took her down to his own cabin, with its bathroom.

'It's beautiful,' Ealasaid enthused, running her fingers along the beaded panelling.

'It's Canadian maple,' he informed her.

Charles Straven never did anything without planning. He wasn't the type of stockbroker who invested his own or other people's money on a hunch. Instead he studied trends and only when he was satisfied that there would be a satisfactory return would he make a commitment. Ever since this young woman had brought him his first plate of soup in the Grand Hotel he had been watching her closely. At first the scrutiny had been entirely physical. As she walked away with his empty plate he had studied the swaying hips in the black skirt. When he started conversing with her he had assessed her personality, concluding that she would be loyal and discreet, which were among the reasons – secondary to her comptometer skills – he had offered her a job in his office.

The truth was that he had made an unhappy marriage. He had proposed to Gladys Davidson, not out of love, but because her father was a prominent stockbroker in Glasgow, and an alliance of his family firm with hers would be financially advantageous. There had been no children and his wife spent most of her time having coffee or shopping with her friends. Some nights his supper was served by their housekeeper. After ten years of marriage they occupied separate bedrooms and took their holidays separately. His wife didn't like boats and flew to their villa in Spain for most of the summer with a succession of friends as house guests.

Charles Straven knew that his attraction towards his comptometer operator went beyond sexual desire. His love for her grew when he was apart from her and as his yacht tacked up the Sound, he realised that by giving her a job in his office he had made her attractive to other men, because now she dressed well. The danger was that one of the young men in the office would invite her out and start a relationship with her. The stockbroker knew that the age gap was great – nearly thirty years – but that he had the advantage over men of her own age group of having money to take her places. He also knew that he had to move quickly, which is why he had planned his tactics – in the same way as he did for a yacht race on the Clyde – as he tacked up the Sound to the bay where he was to meet Ealasaid.

Now, as planned, he had her in his cabin, with only the two of them aboard. Ealasaid was standing, looking through the porthole at the view of the town when he moved behind her and put his arms round her waist. He felt his employee stiffen but she didn't turn round and push him away. Ealasaid didn't know what to do. Was this another sign of affection, like the embrace when they met on the pier? She decides to stand there, as if she's still admiring the view, but he can feel the quickening of her heart against his arm under her breast. He drops his arms, turns her round gently by the shoulders and immediately kisses her on the mouth.

Why doesn't Ealasaid break away and run up the steps on to the deck in distress? Because, at the back of her mind she has known since first serving him in the Grand Hotel that she's attracted to him. The age gap isn't a deterrent – after all, there's more than twenty years between her parents. Her father has always been elderly to her, so she's comfortable with men more than twice her age. When her employer lays her back gently on the bed she struggles a little, then surrenders. This is different from her seduction by the Italian waiter in the Hebridean Hotel where she used to work as a skivvy. He had used stolen wine to take her virginity. But that doesn't have to be defended now and besides, her employer's hands are gentle and unhurried. She has learned from experience that sexual intercourse can have consequences, so she lies still while he rolls on the contraceptive which is within convenient reach in the bedside drawer.

Charles Straven has no idea that the woman underneath him has had previous experience of sex. He believes that he is taking her virginity, which is why his movements are so gentle. Afterwards he lies behind her, clasping her round the waist as she stares through the porthole up to the Hebridean Hotel. She can identify the window behind which she washed the dishes and wonders how she has gone from there, via Glasgow, to lying in bed with a man in the bay, a man who is now fondling her breasts in a most gentle and pleasurable way.

'I love you,' the voice behind assures her.

She doesn't answer. Instead she reaches behind and lays her hand on his thigh, which rouses him again. Charles Straven has never before experienced the emotions that are now sweeping him: desire, satisfaction, love are mingled in this wonderful sensation of peace and fulfilment and he knows that he is never going to let this young woman go.

'I wish we could sail away by ourselves for the rest of the

holiday, leaving the crew behind,' he tells her.

'Where would we go?' she asks, taken with the thought.

'We would sail west, to anchor off uninhabited islands where we could sunbathe naked on the deck and swim in the sea. We would go ashore and light a fire for a barbecue and cook the fish we caught.'

She doesn't ask him why this idyllic voyage isn't possible. She knows that he has a wife, because she's seen her once in the office, a thin, severe looking woman in a fitted costume, with shoes matching the crocodile skin handbag over her arm. She passed Ealasaid in the corridor but didn't acknowledge her.

Her new lover rose and ran the complicated shower for Ealasaid, assuming that she wanted to wash the blood of her seduction from her thighs, though he didn't look for it. She stood under the many tingling jets, soaping herself from the fragrant Floris bar, then standing like a child as he dried her with the large snowy towel. Rubbing her down made him want her again, so they spent another half hour on the bed before she zipped herself back into the blue trousers and tied on the yachting shoes.

'I want to take you to dinner tonight,' he proposes. 'Where would you like to go?'

Ealasaid knows that it's risky, dining alone with a stranger in a town where everyone knows her and where tongues exaggerate stories as they pass them on. On the other hand, why should anyone assume that she's having an affair with a man so much older than herself?

'I'd like to have dinner in the Hebridean Hotel.'

This is a risky choice, dining in the hotel where she used

to work. But the afternoon in bed on the yacht has changed Ealasaid. When she gave herself to the Italian waiter it was an act of shame, because it had been lust, not love, on both sides. But this is different. She knows that her emotions are powerfully involved with this courteous man, who was so gentle and considerate with her. She doesn't care what people will say about her, once it becomes known that she dined with a strange man in the Hebridean Hotel. It's what her parents will think if the gossip reaches them, so she decides to tell them in advance.

'Where are you going?' her mother asks as she emerges from her room in one of her new summer dresses.

'I met the man I work for in the street this morning. He's on a yacht and he asked me to dinner in the Hebridean Hotel.'

Ealasaid couches her statement in such a way that her parents don't doubt that there will be others in the party. In fact they are impressed that their daughter is held in such high esteem that she has been invited to dine with her employer.

As Ealasaid walked along the top of the town in the balmy evening in her new comfortable shoes, she recalled wet mornings when she had made the same journey in heavy footwear to begin the day's work at the scullery sink. Instead of going down the cement steps to the back entrance, she pushed confidently through the swing door and into the hall. Her lover was waiting for her in the cocktail bar. When he asked her what she would like to drink she chose a sherry, though she had never drunk one in her life and when he asked 'sweet or dry?' she asked for the former, because it seemed safer.

In her previous life in the hotel, Ealasaid had had her meals in the drab staffroom below with Peter the barman, who had a serious drink problem and whose morning restorative was Drambuie topped with ice cream. He was watching her with bewilderment as she sat with Charles Straven among the residents having their pre-prandial drinks and talking about what they did that day.

'I've been coming to this hotel for more than twenty years,' Ealasaid's escort recalled.

'And I probably washed your dinner plates,' she informed him, now comfortable with telling him this.

'How did a clever woman like you come to be working in a scullery?' he asked, intrigued.

'Because I left school at sixteen and there were no other jobs in the town. They asked me to stay on to take my Highers, but I had to earn money to help my parents. The other thing was that the hotel is open all the year round, so it was a secure job, a lot easier in the off-season because there weren't so many meals then.'

'Didn't you ever wish you'd stayed on at school?'

'Oh yes. I can remember one morning in October when I was coming down the brae to go to work and a girl who had been in my class passed me in a car and waved. She was being taken down to the boat to go to Glasgow to start university, and I felt very envious.'

'You can still go to university,' her lover pointed out. 'You can go to a college and study for your Highers, then apply to Glasgow University. I'd be very happy to pay for you.'

'It's very generous of you, but I'm contented, working the comptometer.'

Bella the head waitress came through to tell them that their table was ready. She was taken aback and bewildered to see that Charles Straven (whom she had served for years) was accompanied by the former scullery maid.

'How are you, Bella?' Ealasaid asked.

'I'm fine. And you?'

'Very well,' she informed her former workmate as she followed her through to the window table that the stockbroker was always allocated because he was such a generous tipper.

'You'll never guess who's in there and who she's with,' Bella announced to the staff in the scullery, her back to the door.

Ealasaid isn't nervous as she chooses from the menu. She decides that she'll have duck because once, when one meal too many came up from the kitchen, she had been allowed to share it with another member of staff and remembered the succulence of the dark breast meat. Her lover orders lobster. Ealasaid sees a waiter approaching with the wine list under his arm. She recognises Carlo and drops her eyes when he reaches their table and waits while her escort makes his selection.

'Would you like some wine?'

'No thank you,' she tells him, her eyes still on the pristine tablecloth as she waits for her seducer to move away. He has been brought back for the season, having signed a paper to the effect that if he has to leave for any reason, he will have to pay his own fare home.

Straven orders a bottle of quality white and the waiter disappears to fetch it from the subterranean cellar from which he stole the bottle the previous year. Ealasaid won't relax until he has returned with the bottle to ask the purchaser to taste it and then places it in a bucket on a stand beside Straven's chair. She is sitting facing the window. She has never appreciated the full panorama of the beauty of the bay before because her small window next door was always obscured by steam and her hair was over her eyes. The bay is full of yachts of all sizes and beyond, a waterfall spills over rock. She looks at her hands and sees how smooth the skin has become, now that they are no longer immersed in hot water and abrasive soap, the scourer breaking her nails. She looks at her yacht shoes and for an instant doubts that these are her own feet. How has she come to be sitting in this dining-room, having a starter of moist leaves and black olives placed in front of her by intrigued Bella? When the wine bottle is dredged from its slushy ice by her seducer she puts her hand over her glass and pours herself water.

Her escort clinks his glass against her. He doesn't articulate the toast, but she knows that it's for the bond between them. She is now his mistress. This fact takes some swallowing, with the cool water. Is this a position of humiliation and betrayal of the values she was brought up with? She doesn't think so, because the man opposite her gave her the opportunity to leave the dining-room of the Grand Hotel and he was gentle with her in the cabin of his yacht in the bay below. She doesn't feel exploited because she trusts him and is attracted to him.

But she also knows that her companion is married, and that his wife should really be occupying the chair she's sitting in and eating these succulent leaves with their sharp dressing. He hasn't told her very much about his marriage, except to say that 'my wife and I have never really got on. I'm not blaming her, you understand: it's because we have separate interests and opposite personalities. She's a much more sociable person than I am. She loves a dinner party, whereas I prefer to be sitting in my study with a book.'

When the duck came it was so tender that Ealasaid wondered if the chef (whom she knew and who had probably been informed of her presence in the dining-room) had made a special effort. She followed this with a summer pudding of mouth-watering fruits and then her host took her arm through to the conservatory where a tray of coffee had been placed on one of the glass-topped cane tables. Ealasaid had enjoyed the attentive service and superior cuisine of the evening and as she watched Straven lighting a cigar she knew that she could become used to such luxury.

'Tell me about your family,' he requested.

She told him frankly, because she was unashamed and uninhibited. Her father came from a crofting family that had managed to evade the widespread clearances on the island in the middle of the nineteenth century. He had trained as a stonemason and had helped to build and extend some of the big houses on the island, but had fallen from scaffolding and damaged his back. There had been no compensation and he had had to retire from his occupation.

'My mother and I have had to help on the croft when his back gets bad,' Ealasaid informed her listener withour rancour.

'How did you fit it in with working in the hotel?' he wondered.

'Before I left for work I let the cow out, and when I got back in the evening I milked it. My mother fed the hens. When I went to Glasgow a neighbour helped her.'

Charles Straven's admiration for her fortitude and uncomplaining nature increased his love for Ealasaid. He had already decided that he wanted their relationship to be a permanent one, but was well aware of the risks, in the same way as he was aware of the risks of investing in new and untried stocks. The most serious threat to his happiness was from his wife. If she found out that he had a mistress more than half her age, she would make big trouble, so in Glasgow the relationship was going to have to be kept secret – and in particular in the office, where there were people who would inform his wife if they suspected a liaison between the senior partner and the comptometer operator.

But he isn't going to discuss future arrangements with his new lover tonight. He's content to relax in the wicker chair, to inhale his Romeo y Julieta cigar while appreciating her beauty as she sits against the backdrop of the bay, her hands folded on her lap. He wishes he were an artist to record her repose. Ealasaid is as calm and contented as she looks. She likes the company of this caring man and knows that, if she could take him home, her mother would like him. But her parents, both being faithful church attenders, no matter the weather, would be horrified that she had taken up with a married man. This was something she was going to have to reconcile with her own faith, because she knew there would be times of doubt and guilt.

One reason she liked this man opposite her in the warm conservatory above the massed yachts was because he gave her a confidence in herself which she had never possessed before. She was now doing complicated shares calculations on the comptometer which she hadn't imagined she was capable of and he had arranged that she was to have tuition in the fundamentals of stockbroking from one of the partners. This wasn't the plan of a man who was exploiting her.

They went for a walk across the golf course attached to the hotel and sat on a bench overlooking the placid Sound, watching a late yacht motoring in from the Outer Isles under bare poles in the windless evening. They kissed passionately before they went down the brae, parting at the junction. He would have loved to have taken her with him on the next leg of his cruise, out to Barra, but the crew would talk.

'I'll see you in ten days time in Glasgow,' he told her as he took his leave.

Ealasaid spent the rest of her holiday helping on the croft and sitting talking in Gaelic with her parents, telling them about her life in the city and assuring them that she attended church every Sunday. She told them that she had joined a Gaelic choir, which would compete in the Mod in October.

'You haven't met anyone?' her mother enquired.

'What do you mean?'

'I mean, a nice young man.'

'There's time enough for that,' her husband interrupted testily.

At the end of her first week back in the office, Charles Straven sent for her.

'I'm going to take you out for dinner tonight. I want to discuss something with you.'

He picked her up in his impressive car outside the YWCA and drove through to Edinburgh to the Doric Restaurant in Market Street.

'I'd like you to move,' he opened the conversation after

they had ordered from the menu.

'From the comptometer desk?' she queried, puzzled.

'No. From your present lodgings.'

'Where would I go?' she asked apprehensively. She was happy in the YWCA, which had given her shelter when she had first arrived in Glasgow and where she had made friends.

'Somewhere where I can come to see you. I have a property in the west end which I'd like you to use. It's in a very good street and it's lying empty.'

He realised that there was no delicate way of putting this proposal. Did her doubtful expression as she sat opposite him in the Edinburgh restaurant imply that a former mistress, now dismissed, must have occupied his flat? The truth was that on his first day back in the office he had gone out to look at property for sale. He knew that it was too risky to buy a flat in a block, because neighbours could see his coming and going. By that evening had put in an offer for a coach house in the leafy upmarket area of Cleveden. It was separated from the main house by a high wall, thus ensuring complete privacy. Another attraction was that it came fully furnished, having been occupied by an elderly woman who had been moved into a nursing home. The house was expensive, but he could afford to write a cheque for the amount.

He brought in a company to clean the carpets and curtains, then took Ealasaid to see her new abode. She was overwhelmed by its elegance and amenities. It had been owned by a retired doctor of traditional tastes in furnishings and décor. The sofas and chairs in the lounge were covered in patterns of fruit and most of the furniture – including a piano, which Straven had purchased with all the rest – was

176   Maclay Days

mahogany. French windows gave access to the small secluded garden, where a bronze figure of Pan shed water through the pipes at his mouth into a basin.

'What do you think?' asked the stockbroker, anxious about her silence.

'It's beautiful,' she enthused, opening the door of the lighted fridge as though she were inspecting a shrine. She touched the plates of the Aga and admired the willow-patterned blue china on the Welsh dresser.

They went into the main bedroom, its window overlooking the garden, material with fruits gathered into a canopy above the headboard of the bed. The old doctor had been a spinster, but Straven had had the single bed replaced by a double that morning. Ealasaid sat on the sprung mattress, not knowing what to say. She was grateful for his consideration in providing her with such a place, but she also saw how extravagant it was, compared to her own home on the island and her room in the YWCA. For the first time she felt like a kept woman.

'If there are things you don't like we can have them changed,' he offered.

She rose and put her arms round his neck and he went to undo the cords holding back the heavy curtains before laying her on the new bed.

'I hope you'll be happy here,' he said as he lay beside her, utterly relaxed in the summer dusk.

'Why would I not be?' she asked, touching his face with her fingertips.

'You'll be able to get a bus from down on Great Western Road into the office,' he informed her.

He drove her into the city so that she could fetch her case from the YWCA and on the way back to the coachhouse he collected an order from a curry house. They sat down together at the circular table in the dining room for their first meal together in the new place. The rice was moist and fragrant, the curry mild, full of appetising spices and they finished with sorbets contained in two scooped-out lemons.

'To your new home,' he proposed, touching his glass of beer against hers of water. But he knew that it was as much his home as hers and that in a very short time he would consider it to be his main home, the Kilmalcolm mansion a place he had to return to reluctantly each night, to be confronted by his angry wife asking where he had been.

'I've had meetings.'

'Where?' Gladys demanded to know.

'In the Central Hotel.'

'So that's why you didn't answer the phone in your office. I think you were somewhere else.'

For a moment he feared that she had put a private detective on his trail, until she said: 'I hope you haven't got your father's weakness.'

His father had been a compulsive poker player, losing untold thousands in games in grubby flats where the most important item was the table the players were grouped round.

'I have no interest in gambling, Gladys,' he told his wife wearily. 'My main interest as I've told you so many times is making money so that we can have a comfortable life.' The last monthly account to Fraser Sons which he had paid for her had amounted to three hundred pounds, for two costumes, but he doesn't cast that up tonight because he wants to retire to his study in peace with a cigar, rather than start a quarrel which will end in her screaming at him and slamming a succession of doors on her retreat to her own quarters.

Instead of reading one of the many yachting books from his shelves he took out the packet of photographs he had developed. They were taken on the deck of his yacht and show his lover standing against the backdrop of the Hebridean Hotel, a hand holding one of the stays supporting the mast. He thinks she looks very beautiful and having studied the photo for five minutes, locks the packet away in his desk and takes a stamp album down from the shelf to add expensive new purchases, moistening the folded flimsy hinge with his tongue before affixing it to the back of the Penny Black.

Their lives fall into a pleasing pattern. Ealasaid leaves the office at five o' clock and takes a bus along Great Western Road. Straven waits until six before switching off his desk light. He goes down in the lift to his car in its private space and drives out to Cleveden Road, parking a hundred yards down from Ealasaid's new residence because someone could recognise his distinctive vehicle with one of the first personalised number plates in Renfrewshire. She will be in the kitchen, an apron knotted round her hips as she prepares their supper. At home she helped with the cooking, but that was basic fare, mostly what they grew or reared themselves on the croft, or what came from the sea. But now she has become more adventurous. She bought a cookery book in John Smith in St Vincent Street and tonight she's trying spaghetti for the first time. The long pale strands are in the simmering pot and she's chopping a tomato on the wooden board, scored by the blades of the previous owner of the property who swore by a diet of vegetables. He comes in behind her, placing the bottle of superior red wine on the table and putting his arms round her waist to nuzzle her neck. Then he picks up a segment of tomato and eats it before setting the table in the dining-room.

Ealasaid loves her new home. She loves the luxury of being able to run a bath in the morning, whereas on the island, before going out to work in the hotel, she had to wash at the scullery sink. She loves having a choice of clothes on the spacious rail and is slowly building up a selection of stylish shoes at the bottom of the wardrobe that glides open to her touch. He won't raise the suspicions and jealousy of his office manager by giving his comptometer operator a rise in salary to help with the expenses of her new home. Instead he leaves banknotes in the drawer in the bedroom. And he pays the utility bills on the property. Though she never asks, he makes sure that she wants for nothing, but he tries to keep his generosity discreet.

The truth is (though he hasn't yet said this to Ealasaid) that if he could get a divorce from his wife, he would marry her as soon as it was granted. But he knows that if he asked to be freed from his unsatisfactory marriage, Gladys will go about the city, bad-mouthing him to his friends and business acquaintances, telling them that he has lost his sense of judgement by falling for an ignorant office girl from the Islands and that he can no longer be trusted with the investment capital of clients. It saddens him that they will have to share that large house in Kilmalcolm for the foreseeable future, when he could be happy with Ealasaid and could start a family with her, something that he has always wanted. It wasn't barrenness that made his wife adamant against having children. She complained that it would curtail her freedom to see her friends and besides, as she admitted to him, she didn't have maternal instincts and would rather be riding her horse through the lanes of Renfrewshire than wheeling a pram.

Ealasaid trawls the dripping spaghetti from the pot on to the blue plates and they sit down facing each other. He's expert at twirling the strands on to his fork because he has taken many holidays in Italy and has even considered buying a house there. But this is Ealasaid's first encounter with the staple food of the Italians and they both laugh as the strands fall off the fork. He moistens his napkin at his mouth and leans over to dab the red stains from her chin.

While she is doing the washing-up, he filters coffee that was ground fresh for him that morning in Matthew Algie's in Cadogan Street and carries the tray through to the lounge. He has yet another present for her tonight and hands her a small black box. She springs the catch to a silver Iona cross lying in a bed of satin.

'It's beautiful,' she enthuses, lifting it out on its slim silver chain.

'It belonged to my mother,' he explains. 'She was wearing it when she died.'

It forms part of his mother's jewellery collection which he didn't pass to his wife and which he keeps in the locked drawer in his library in Kilmalcolm. Ealasaid realises the emotional significance of the gift as he loops the chain round her neck and closes the delicate clasp. She feels the cold silver on her skin.

Another evening, another gift. This time it was a large brown envelope.

'I want you to keep this safe and if anything happens to me you've to open it.'

'Don't say such a thing,' she pleads fearfully, having been brought up in a superstitious household where to speak of misfortune encourages it.

'I want you to do this for me,' he asks and she puts the envelope at the bottom of her underwear drawer.

Their relationship continued smoothly and discreetly. He had supper there three evenings a week and on Sunday he drove her a safe distance beyond the city, dining her in small country restaurants where they could hold hands. Every summer his student crew sailed his yacht through the Crinan Canal to the west coast and Ealasaid would be waiting for him on the stone pier in the bay of her home island. The long established ritual was that they made love on the yacht before going up the hill to the Hebridean Hotel. Bella the head waiter was slower on her feet now, her service less sharp and sometimes she forgot an order. Carlo the waiter was home in Italy, with his own little restaurant in Rome and a bambino.

When Ealasaid's father died in his chair one autumn, she went home to arrange the funeral and afterwards provided refreshments for the mourners in the dining-room of the Hebridean Hotel. She went among the tables in her smart black costume, thanking people in Gaelic for attending. But she was troubled as she took her mother's arm home. She felt that she couldn't leave her alone on the island. On the other hand, if she came to stay with her in Glasgow, Charles wouldn't be able to visit any more. Was she going to have to choose between the two?

'It's good of you to think of me, but I couldn't live in Glasgow,' her mother told her. 'I was born here and I want to die here, to stay as long as I'm able in this house because it has so many happy memories for me of your father and you.'

Ealasaid knew that she couldn't move back to the island, not only because there wasn't suitable work for her newly acquired skills, but because her life was in Glasgow. She arranged for a woman to come in once a week to clean the house for her mother and to bring up shopping from the town.

Ealasaid returned to the ritual of her life in the city, to what was in effect a married existence in the coachhouse in Cleveden. She had learned to eat spaghetti like an Italian. One evening Charles brought in a bottle of Asti Spumante, easing out the cork with his thumbs and pouring the frothing wine into two tall glasses.

'What are we celebrating?' she asked.

'Being together.'

But when she hands him her glass she has taken only a sip. After his second glass she reminded him that he had to drive home.

'I'm staying here tonight.'

He finished the bottle and drank a sizeable goblet of Courvoisier brandy before they went to bed. It was the first time they had slept together for a night and she put her arms round the warmth of his body. She wanted to say *'won't your wife miss you?'* But she didn't want to destroy the peace and contentment of their bed.

He woke her up at 2 a.m. to tell her that he had a pain in his chest.

'It'll be indigestion,' she told him, massaging the area.

But when he began to cry out with the pain she went through to phone an ambulance. It only took fifteen minutes, but when she let the crew in, they found the stockbroker dead in her bed. Though Ealasaid was distraught, she knew that his wife had to be informed, but she didn't even know her late lover's home address and had to ask directory enquiries to find Straven in Kilmalcolm.

Gladys Straven arrived in her own car an hour later, having put on her make-up.

'So that's what he's been doing when he hasn't come home – consorting with prostitutes?' she said as Ealasaid let her in.

The widow arranged to have the body removed to a mortuary and then she rounded on Ealasaid.

'Is this your house?'

'No. It's Charles's.'

'Mr Straven to you. I want you out by the morning, otherwise my lawyer will get a court order to evict you. And another thing. If you breathe one word to anyone that you were my husband's floozy, I'll ruin you. Where do you work?'

'In Charles's office.'

'You're out of a job now. And don't dare try to attend the funeral service.'

Ealasaid sat weeping for a long time after the vengeful woman had slammed the door. She wasn't weeping for herself, but for her lost lover, for the years of happiness. She had no regrets at having given herself body and soul to a man so many years her senior – a man who had always been so kind and considerate towards her. But now she had no job and had nowhere to stay. She would have to go back to the island, to try to get work on the reception desk in the Hebridean Hotel.

She went through to the kitchen and sat with the empty bottle of Asti Spumante in her arms. Then she remembered what he had said to her and she went through to the bedroom. She had forgotten about the large envelope, but when she retrieved it she found that it contained two documents. One was the title deeds to the coachhouse in her name, the other a letter stating that Charles Straven had lodged twenty thousand pounds in her name in a city bank.

The following morning the widow's lawyer appeared at the door to ask her why she hadn't vacated the property. She showed him the title deeds and he went away to report to an infuriated Mrs Straven.

'You're going to challenge this in the court,' she instructed the lawyer. 'Charles couldn't have been in sound mind when he signed away the property to that slut.'

'I wouldn't do that,' he cautioned. 'The deeds are in order, and there's no evidence that your husband was mentally ill in any way. Challenge it and you'll bring most unwelcome publicity on your head. And the defendant will be awarded costs against you.'

Ealasaid decided that she wasn't going to go back to the island. Instead she persuaded another stockbroking firm to take her on, since she had experience. She used her late lover's money to continue living in the property. His widow would never be aware that he had left his mistress a substantial sum.

Entitlement

When her mother had a fall, Ealasaid arranged for her to go into the small hospital that had been recently built on the island and visited her as often as she could.

The firm with which Ealasaid served her stockbroking apprenticeship was so impressed with her that they retained her on staff and within a year she was handling substantial portfolios for clients. Within three years she was a partner.

At her mother's funeral she broke with the convention that females were not allocated cords by insisting that she was to get the head one. After she had lowered her parent into the island soil, she asked the minister to announce that there would be refreshments in the Hebridean Hotel and that everyone was most welcome.

13. Protection

'I won't be here tonight,' Moira Dunsyre announced casually to her roommate as they were having supper in Wolfson Hall. 'I'll be staying with a friend.'

'Have you told the warden?' Marsaili asked.

'I don't think that's necessary. You'll cover for me.'

This request left the veterinary science student uneasy. Most nights Moira hadn't been coming in until late and Marsaili saw no signs that she was doing any studying. In fact, her roommate left a letter lying around. It was from her professor, warning her that 'non-attendance at classes means that you will not qualify for a class ticket in order to proceed towards a degree.'

There was something else that was even more worrying. Moira seemed to have acquired an extensive wardrobe, though she was always complaining that she was short of money. Marsaili suspected that she had become the mistress of a wealthy man. She watched her friend preparing for her overnight stay. The small wardrobe they had each been allocated wasn't large enough to accommodate Moira's increasing collection, so she kept her newly acquired garments in a suitcase under her bed. Down on her knees, she lifted out a top which Marsaili hadn't seen before. Moira removed the price tag from the spangled garment with her teeth.

'They should give us a decent mirror,' she complained as she regarded herself in the small glass. 'What do you think?'

'It's very nice,' Marsaili said sincerely.

The myriad gold discs looked like miniature coins that had been painstakingly sewn on the black material.

'We're going out for a meal.'

Marsaili didn't ask who the *We* referred to. She watched Moira packing a white leather vanity case with clothes and cosmetics, of which she had acquired such a wide range that part of Marsaili's surface had been appropriated. She lifted down a box from on top of the wardrobe and removed a pair of gold-coloured slippers from their tissue wrapping. It crossed Marsaili's mind that her roommate might be a skilled shoplifter. But if that were the case, what person was going to admire the stolen garments tonight?

'Take care,' Marsaili called as Moira reached the door. She turned and gave her roommate a look which Marsaili would later puzzle over. Was it pride, or fear?

However, she was grateful for the peace of the room, and as she studied she didn't have to have the window open on the bitter night in order to dispel the cigarette smoke. It was also good not to have the occupant of the next bed restless in her sleep.

Moira didn't tell her roommate that this was a very special occasion. She was picked up outside the hall of residence by a red Triumph Spitfire, driven by the same Sean who had danced so spectacularly with her at the Halloween Ball in the Locarno. Tonight he isn't dressed as King Robert the Bruce, but has on a well-cut dark lounge suit bought from Mann the Tailor in Sauchiehall Street and into which had been inserted extra pads for his shoulders. The shoes on the pedals of the Spitfire – one of the first in Glasgow – are Italian, with golden chains.

When they fled the famine in Ireland in the mid-1800s, Sean Duffy's family, with hundreds of others, had brought across to Glasgow a kist containing a Bible, a fiddle and already sewn shrouds. They squatted in some of the worst slums of Europe and queued at the gates of the shipyards in search of work, but their names and their Catholicism told against them. Some of then changed their names, but not their religion. In the Gorbals the eight Duffy children played in the squalid streets and slept four to a bed, heads to feet. When they were told that they were being rehoused in the newly built scheme of Easterhouse, they had gone down on their knees in the kitchen to give thanks for their deliverance.

The father was grateful to get a job on a building site but Sean had bigger ambitions. He was bright enough to go to university but decided that he wanted to earn money as soon as possible and became a clerk in a betting office, where his ability to calculate complicated winning accumulators in his head impressed his boss, who made him the shop manager at the age of twenty. But when he arrived at work in a Triumph Herald the boss became worried, because he knew he wasn't paying him enough to buy a car and the sharp suits he came to work in. An investigation showed that Sean was laying bets for himself after the horses had passed the post. When the owner of the betting shop said he was calling in the police, Sean put a restraining hand over his on the phone, advising him that something might happen to his shop.

This was the basis for his protection racket and soon he was receiving regular weekly payments from a dozen betting shops. Business boomed so much that he had to take on half a dozen out-of-work employees from Easterhouse. The only qualifications demanded were the ability to threaten and the strength to carry out an attack should a payment be refused. One betting shop owner lost an eye for the sake of thirty pounds. Sean also began offering protection to other businesses, notably restaurants, because of the risk of fire.

The Triumph Spitfire in which Moira is sitting in her finery didn't start out from Easterhouse, because it would have been vandalised in the street and also because Sean had moved to an area of the city more befitting a successful entrepreneur who had no office, no account books. He has come from his flat in the west end, which is tastefully furnished and has a door entry system.

'Where are we going?' Moira asks above the radio on which Mantovani is playing 'Moon River.'

'It's a surprise.'

They drive past ballrooms, brilliantly lit for the evening's business, and restaurants where waiters are checking the geometry of the cutlery. Glasgow in the early 1960s is a vibrant city of many races and many tastes and at the corner of Gordon Street, Moira glimpses a woman in a short skirt in a doorway.

Her escort parks the sports car on Sauchiehall Street and leads her by the hand into the Argyll Arcade, past the windows of jewellers flaring with rings and pendants. He leads her up the stairs into Sloans Restaurant. It's a surprising choice for a young man who considers himself to be trendy, but Sloans is the oldest and one of the most respected restaurants in Glasgow, much patronised, especially at lunchtime, by successful businessmen whose bowlers and umbrellas are conveyed to brass hooks by waitresses with whom they are on first name terms and who know to bring them gin and bitters as aperitifs, over which they discuss the morning's trading on the nearby Stock Exchange.

Sean likes this restaurant because of its ambience and because it confers respectability on him. Also, he admires the decoration on the ceilings, having been interested in art at school.

They are led to a table in a shaded corner by the head waiter and Moira is impressed when he is called 'Mr Duffy' and she is addressed as Madam. The menus they are brought are the size of folio books and after she has chosen halibut and he a steak, her host asks the waiter's advice about the compatibility of wines with fish and meat.

'How are you getting on at university?' Sean asks when their order is taken to the kitchen.

'Fine.'

This isn't the truth. She's in serious trouble for her indolence.

'That's good. You know, I'm proud of you,' he tells her, and his hand covers hers on the immaculate white cloth.

She's ashamed that she's deceiving this attractive and

attentive young man. What she loves about him most is his ability to switch – from being a formidable king with battle-axe on the sparkling floor of the Locarno, to a suave escort under this gilded roof, with sophisticated people dining around them.

He reaches into his pocket with the same deft care as when he's confronted with a recalcitrant client and has to produce his calling card, an old-fashioned open razor that belonged to his grandfather. He places the small black box by Moira's side plate and springs the catch with his thumb.

Moira is looking wide-eyed at diamonds, a small fire kindled in a satin bed. The only jewellery she possesses is cheap paste, but she knows that what is sparkling beside her plate is real quality. She also knows that it's an engagement ring.

'It's too early for this, Sean.'

It isn't that she doesn't love him; but she knows that this will be a further distraction from her studies. She can't wear an engagement ring in front of her roommate or her lecturers.

'Why is it too early?' he asks, the first time she's heard a hint of impatience in his voice.

'Because – '

'Yes?'

But the cluster of diamonds seems to be mesmerising her and she stretches out her fingers.

'Wrong hand,' he corrects her

She laughs and extends the other one and he loosens the gem from its satin bed and slides it up her finger.

'A perfect fit,' he says.

He has always been good at judging such details. As for

the ring, which is attracting admiration from other diners as she moves her hand, he didn't select it from a tray in one of the jewellers in the Arcade below.

He chose a jeweller in a less conspicuous location because he knew that the owner would be serving behind the counter.

Sean asked to see his top-of-the-range engagement rings, and when the man had produced the tray from the safe in the back premises, the customer made his selection carefully.

'How much is this one?' he enquired reasonably, holding it up like a spark between two fingers.

The jeweller retrieved the ring and looked at the small figures on the label with his naked eye.

'Six hundred pounds.'

The customer took back the ring and held it on his palm, as if weighing it.

'Two years protection.'

'What do you mean?' the proprietor asked uneasily, his hand out for the ring.

But he didn't get it back. Instead he received two possibilities: either the ring was given as advance payment for protection for the shop, or else the proprietor would start to have many problems.

As a Jewish youth in Hitler's Germany, he had seen his parents' jewellery shop smashed and ransacked by uniformed thugs. They had sold their stock for a tenth of the value in order to get out of the country and had had to start again in Glasgow. His parents were both dead and he had two children at university, one of them studying forensic science, the other law. He could go to the police with this extortion threat, but he knew from the face of the customer across the counter that his shop would still suffer, so he reached under the counter and produced a box for the ring.

Sean asked the waiter in Sloans to offer glasses of champagne round the dining-room to celebrate the engagement and after they had toasted the couple, diners came up to the table to offer their congratulations. By the end of the meal (on the house because of the special occasion, and because Mr Duffy was a valued customer) they had drunk a considerable amount between them, but he still drove her in the Triumph Spitfire, dancers on their way home from the Barrowland having to jump out of the way. The powerful motor was left to cool in the underground garage while they ascended to the top storey in the elevator panelled in fake marble. The view of the luminous extent of the city from the picture window was spectacular.

'That's my hall of residence down there,' Moira pointed out as they sat with a night-cap.

She thinks of her roommate, sitting in peace studying a text book on the care of small animals. She knows that Marsaili is an upright young woman, honest and sincere, dedicated to her course, the kind of person one could turn to in trouble. She's sure that her roommate hasn't surrendered her virginity and that she would be very wary of a man in a flashy sports car, with plenty of money to spend. As she sits there, with the ring on her finger and her lover impatient to go to bed, she knows – not for the first time – that she has sold and cheapened herself for worldly goods.

She doesn't enjoy sex with Sean now. It was fabulous at the beginning, but it's become a service she's providing for him. He falls asleep immediately after and sleeps with his mouth shut, giving nothing away from his dreams. Some nights, with his face lit up by the luminescence of the city, she thinks that he looks sinister, but that's probably her own imagination. She doesn't even know what business he's in, but he tells her that it's 'lucrative' and when she asks about his family, he claims that they live in an old-established villa on the south side. What strikes her about this apartment (his word) is the lack of photographs, not even of himself, and the only mirror in the place is an insufficient one in the bathroom. The furniture is dark wood and leather, but stylish. He has urged her to move out of the hall of residence, in with him, with the enticement that he'll get her a piano, but she resists because she likes her own space. She senses that if she comes here, her freedom will be curtailed and that he'll expect her to sit studying when he's at business. She knows that she's falling further and further behind and that soon she'll be called into the professor's room and told that her lack of class tickets prevents her from proceeding to a degree. She'll have to leave and Sean will be annoyed, which is why she must get down to studying, to redeem the situation before it's too late. Perhaps she should sit studying beside Marsaili in the evenings, she tells herself before sleep overtakes her.

Moira didn't wear her ring in the hall of residence or at university. Instead she kept it in its black box in the drawer of the room she shared with Marsaili. She began to make a real effort to catch up with her studies and stayed in at night. But Marsaili found this even more off-putting because her roommate was lighting a new cigarette from the stub of the old as she tried to assimilate the theory of music. Also, her lover had purchased a guitar for her and its strumming broke Marsaili's concentration. Her eyes were smarting so much that she couldn't see the page and she knew that she was going to have to consult the reformed music student.

'I'm finding that your smoke's going for my eyes.'

Moira was immediately sympathetic and stubbed out the newly lit cigarette, vowing that it was the last she would smoke in the room.

'I'll go downstairs and find myself a quiet space.'

'I'm sorry – '

'No need to apologise.' She held up a conciliatory hand. 'My mother used to tell me that I could be very selfish.'

Marsaili didn't particularly want an intimate conversation on her roommate's family history, so she returned to the page on the skeleton of a small mammal which she was trying to assimilate. She opened the window for five minutes and the smoke was gone, though its bitter aftermath would linger on walls and fabrics for weeks to come and the guitar would be brought out every evening.

But Moira had difficulty establishing a base for herself in one of the public rooms downstairs. Most of the chairs and tables were taken by women who had come to university with the sole purpose of getting first class degrees and not participating in the social life of hall and campus. There was a room given over to conversation and music in which smoking was permitted, but the radiogram was always on with the latest release. The indolent are sprawled in chairs, smoking as their bare feet on the floorboards keep time with the crooner. Moira would love to take an available chair and light up, but she

Maclay Days

knows that if she doesn't do some studying, she won't survive her first year. As she finds an empty chair at a table in the quiet lounge, she knows that she daren't smoke among those dedicated students, the salad eaters and orange juice imbibers for whom cigarettes are an abomination.

When she phones Sean from the booth he wants to know why she isn't coming out with him.

'Because I have to study.'

'Why?'

'I need to get a degree, to earning my living.'

'No you don't.'

'What – get a degree?'

'Neither. I don't want my wife working. I want her to stay at home and bring up the kids. I'll go out and earn the money.'

This plan makes Moira's heart sink as she stands with the receiver away from her ear. What is she going to say? She loves this man and will probably marry him, but not yet. She wants to enjoy her student years and to get her degree.

'I'll pick you up in half an hour.'

'I can't,' she tells him. 'I've an essay to complete by tomorrow.'

'Half an hour,' he repeats in a commanding tone before putting down the phone.

Now that she has found a work-space and the will to apply herself, she doesn't want to go out, but knows that he'll ring the bell and embarrass her in front of the warden. She's also having her suspicion confirmed that this man with whom she has become involved isn't going to take no for an answer.

She was waiting on the steps in the imitation ocelot jacket he had bought for her when the Triumph glided up.

'Where's the ring?'

Oh God, she's forgotten to put it on in the rush to get ready.

'I took it off to do my nails in case I got polish on the beautiful diamonds.'

'You haven't lost it?'

'I swear I haven't, Sean. Where are we going?'

'For something to eat.'

'But I've already eaten supper.'

'I haven't.'

He didn't tell her that he had had a particularly trying day. One of the bookies who was paying extortion money had suddenly become bold and had refused to put the forty pounds into the collector's gloved hand.

'I'll have to take this up with the boss. He isn't going to be pleased with you.'

'Tell him to fuck off.'

'The boss doesn't like swearing.'

Sean was counting money at the mahogany table in his flat when the collector buzzed, his murky voice announcing through the security phone that he had 'hit a problem'. Sean pressed the button to open the downstairs door and put the takings back into the attaché case, with the other neat wads of bills.

'You should have roughed him up,' the boss rebuked the collector.

'I didn't want to do anything without consulting you.'

'In that case I'd better pay him a visit,' Sean said, playing with his cigarette packet.

The last race was being run over the tannoy as the two

men entered the grimy betting shop, its floor strewn with discarded dreams. There was a security grille between the visitors and the owner as they conducted their conversation.

'I believe you don't want to pay,' Sean said calmly.

'You've got it. Fuck off and don't send round any more of your thugs.'

'I'm going to have to charge you extra for your insolence,' Sean cautioned him.

The door opened behind the two callers and a burly man came in. The collar of his coat was turned up and his hands were thrust into his pockets. Sean recognised him as George Hagan, a former member of the gang to which they had both belonged.

A hand came out of Hagan's pocket with a knife.

'I always wanted to have a go at you, Duffy, you bastard, the way you ordered us about. Go and steal cigarettes for me; go into that Paki's and bring me what's in the till. You never got your hands dirty, did you?'

Sean nodded to his henchman. He opened his long coat to expose the sword hanging from his belt. The design was based on the kind of weapon that the Crusaders would have carried in their campaigns against the infidels. The hilt was elaborate and the blade had been sharpened on a sandstone block driven by a belt. The wielder of the sword had taken fencing lessons in a boys' club in the city, the tutor mistakenly believing that he wanted to become a serious competitor.

The first slash took two fingers away as the knife clattered to the floor.

'Any more, boss?'

'One more.'

So the third finger went, the former owner howling in pain. Sean turned, addressing the shop owner who had been watching in terror from behind the grille and who was now pushing a wad of notes through.

'You'd better phone for an ambulance before he bleeds to death. And if you ever say who did it – '

He parked the car up on the pavement in Exchange Square and took Moira's arm into the Rogano, where he was known. He had already phoned in to ask them to keep him seafood and he snapped the crab's claws to get at the succulent meat as his dining companion had a plate of clam chowder.

'We'll get married in the spring.'

'Sean, I've got to finish my degree and that'll take three more years.'

'OK.'

But her thankful look faded when he continued: 'You can continue studying for your degree and when the baby's born we'll get someone in to look after it while you're at university.'

'Can't we postpone starting a family until I've graduated?' she pleaded.

'Three years is too long,' he replied brusquely.

'Then two. I'll take an ordinary degree.'

'Still too long. I want a family, Moira. Irish Catholics do.'

'But I'm a Protestant,' she said, as if her religious persuasion had just occurred to her.

'You'll turn.'

'My father plays the big drum in an Orange Band.'

He pushed the fork in to get the last of the crab's flesh, the tablecloth littered with its shattered claws.

'You'll turn.'

This is when Moira becomes aware that she's involved with a man she doesn't really know. What exactly does he make his money from? He's never discussed his business with her. He has the smooth hands of a worker at a desk as they roam over her body. She begins to realise that she's in thrall to this domineering male and this frightens her. She's going to have to break with him, but she knows this won't be easy. The waiter offers her a sweet from the laden trolley, but she wants to get back to her quarters.

'When will I see you again?' he asks when he drops her off at the hall.

'I don't know, I have a lot of work to do.'

'Friday night. We'll go to the Locarno,' he says, starting the engine and surging away, leaving her standing without the right of reply.

'You're very pale. Is there something wrong?' Marsaili asks. She has managed to come to terms with the skeleton of the small mammal in the peace of the smoke-free atmosphere.

'No, I'm fine.'

But she can't sleep, thinking about the situation she's in. Of course she was attracted to the glamour and style of the man when she first saw him twisting on the floor of the Locarno as if he had been blessed with extra joints. The next time she saw him, he had changed from a velvet-collared Teddy boy to a suave person in a business suit, with a gold chain on his left wrist. Then that wonderful car which, he told her, he had had on order for six months before it was delivered on a transporter to Glasgow. She had thought he was a person of status because of the deferential way he was shown to his table in restaurants and at the beginning of their romance (she wouldn't use that word now) she had found him considerate. Now she dreaded Friday night. No, she wouldn't go. She realised that he had never given her his phone number but she had been to his flat and the following afternoon, after her classes, she pushed a note through the letterbox, telling him that she couldn't manage Friday night. She knew that she should have had the courage to tell him that she didn't want to see him again, but she feared the consequences of that intimation and decided to stall for time. Perhaps he would lose interest in her and find another partner on the frenetic floor of the Locarno.

'There's someone waiting for you downstairs,' one of the residents came up to tell her on Friday evening as she was practising a Bob Dylan number on her guitar. She had the room to herself because Marsaili was out at a dance at which her brother was playing and she was enjoying a smoke and a magazine.

'Say you can't find me,' she pleaded.

'I've already told him you're in. He's *very* good looking and has a gorgeous car.'

'Tell him I'll be down in ten minutes.'

It was with a heavy heart that Moira lifted a dress from the wardrobe. You had to be in the mood for dancing, to delight in the whole ritual, from applying your make-up to selecting a pair of shoes. Before she went down she stooped to look at her anxious face in the small mirror, asking herself aloud: 'why was I stupid enough to get involved with this man?'

He was sitting in the darkened car, listening to classical

music on the radio when she opened the low door and climbed in.

'Why did you put that note through my door, saying you couldn't come out tonight?'

'Because I have work to do. I'm already in danger of being thrown out of university. I don't have your phone number.'

'You didn't ask for it.'

'You didn't offer it.'

'We need to put this on a better basis. We'll call the banns for Easter, take a honeymoon abroad – you can choose the destination – and work things out for your studies next year.'

'I told you, Sean, I don't want to get married while I'm still a student.'

'At Easter,' he said in a tone that brooked no argument.

That was what made her reach for the door handle, but he leaned across her to prevent her exit.

'No one walks out on me.'

'What does that mean?' she asked fearfully.

But he pushed the car into gear and put his foot down.

Moira didn't enjoy that evening's dancing. It was as if her limbs had turned to lead, but the man opposite her in his Teddy boy costume was squirming down on his sponge soles, the tail of his long jacket brushing the floor. The lights and the noise were giving her a devastating headache and when she went into the Ladies she had to hold on to the taps, because it felt as if the whole ballroom was vibrating. She saw her frightened face in the haze of the mirror but knew that she had nowhere to run to. Wherever she went, that red car would follow her and be outside every door she opened.

He wanted to drive her back to his flat, but when she told

him that she had a 'heavy period', he let her out at the Hall.

Marsaili wakened up when the light was snapped on.

'You look dreadful. What's happened?'

Moira sat down on her roommate's bed and made her confession about her relationship with the mysterious young businessman who drove one of the first Triumph Spitfires in Glasgow and was forcing her into marriage.

'Slavery was abolished a long time ago,' Marsaili reminded her. 'You don't have to marry a person you obviously don't love. Tell him.'

'I've told him, but he won't take no for an answer.'

'But you're not even engaged.'

In response Moira went to her drawer and handed her roommate the small black box. Marsaili sprung the catch on the small fire of precious stones.

'This must have cost a lot of money. What does he do for a living?'

'I don't know. I don't know hardly anything about him. I've been to his flat – his apartment, he calls it – and it's very modern and beautifully furnished. He seems to have plenty of money and takes me to very smart restaurants where he's known.'

'You don't know who you're mixed up with, Moira. Anyone as well off and successful as he seems to be would surely be proud of what he does and would tell you. He may be into some shady business.'

'How do I get away from him?' Moira asked, more frightened than ever.

'You tell him that it's over.'

'But he'll appear here and sit outside in the car until I go out to him.'

'If he comes in here the warden will call the police. That'll deter him, if he's into something outside the law. Write to him.'

'Will you help me compose the letter?'

'If you want. You'd better get some sleep.'

'Do you mind if I have one cigarette to steady my nerves? I'll lean out of the window.'

With Marsaili's help, Moira wrote another letter and after she pushed it through his communal letterbox she was still apprehensive that she wasn't going to get away so easily. She went up to university with a lighter heart and for the first time since her arrival, really paid attention to what she was being taught in the theory of music class and actually went into one of the cubicles for an hour of piano practice. In fact she went back to the hall of residence singing and that evening, to celebrate her release, she and her roommate went down to the University Café where they indulged themselves with coffee and ice cream. There was no sports car outside the door of the Hall when they arrived back, but there was a letter waiting for Moira in the entrance hall. She carried it up to the room and extracted the sheet from the envelope with trembling fingers, and read it out to Marsaili.

Dear Moira,
I was out at business this morning and your letter
was awaiting me when I returned at lunchtime. I

am deeply sorry you feel that we do not have a future together, as I love you and would be proud to have you as my wife. I see now that I have been too impatient about setting a wedding date, but I was worried that I would lose you to the clever competition up at the university. However, I accept your decision and would only ask that you return the ring. It is valuable and so I do not think it is advisable to post it, or to put it through my letterbox. If you come here on Saturday morning you can return it to me and we can take a fond farewell of each other. I wish you every success with your studies, and know that whoever you marry will be a very fortunate man.

With Love,

Sean Duffy

'It's a very well written letter and the handwriting is beautiful,' Marsaili observed. As she listened to its reasonable tone she began to doubt her own analysis of the character of her roommate's lover. Here was old-world courtesy and consideration.

'It's a trick,' Moira averred.

'What's a trick?'

'Asking me to return the ring in person.'

'Well, I suppose that if it's valuable, he doesn't want it put through the letterbox.'

'I could leave it downstairs and tell him to come and collect it,' Moira suggested.

'That would be a good compromise,' Marsaili conceded.

'Do I need to reply to this letter?' Moira asked her adviser.

'I wouldn't. You've already told him you want to break it off.'

So Moira put the small black box into an envelope and wrote in black ink on the outside: Mr Sean Duffy. To Be Collected. But as she was going downstairs she fell into conversation with one of the students from her class and forgot to leave the envelope downstairs. After her first lecture, when she went to the café for a coffee and a smoke, she discovered it in her bag and decided to hand it in on her way back to the Hall in the afternoon.

The man who had three fingers amputated with the sword in the bookmaker's had almost bled to death because the ambulance had been delayed by heavy traffic. The bookmaker was mopping the blood on the linoleum, among crushed betting slips, when the detective came in.

'Who did it to George Hagan?' he asked.

'Is he dead?' the bookmaker wanted to know.

'No, but he lost a lot of blood.' He repeated the question.

'I can describe him, but I can't name him,' the bookie said. 'About five feet ten inches tall, burly, with a scar on his left cheek. He cut the man's fingers off because he was told to do it.'

'Told by whom?' the detective asked.

'If I tell you, will you give me protection?'

'If we think you need it.'

'That's not a very helpful answer.'

'I need to hear a name first before I can ask my superior for protection.'

'He came in with Sean Duffy. He's been getting a regular payment from me, otherwise he says he'll destroy my shop.'

The detective's face showed that he didn't know that name.

'Am I going to get protection?' the bookie asked plaintively.

'I'll let you know once I see what form this man Duffy has.'

But when he went back to the station he couldn't find Duffy's name on the files and took the problem to the Inspector.

'There's an easy way to do this,' the Inspector explained. 'Go to the Infirmary and go through Hagan's clothes, to see if there's an address.'

Mary Hagan was sitting by her husband's bed when the detective came in.

'I told George not to get mixed up with Duffy,' she said, distraught. 'I said: he's far too clever for you and he'll just get you into trouble, but Duffy paid him well. Tainted money. And when they fell out I knew that George was a marked man.'

'Where does Duffy live?'

'In a block of fancy flats in Hyndland. George said he had a lift,' she added in wonder.

Moira buzzed the entry button, and when she had identified herself, a voice invited her to enter. She rose smoothly in the imitation marble lift to the third floor. He was waiting in the foyer and she opened her satchel and handed him the envelope.

'This isn't a very good way of saying goodbye,' he

observed. 'Come in for a minute.'

'I'd rather not.'

'I'm not going to harm you.'

He laid the envelope containing the ring on the dark wood of the table and offered to make coffee for her, but she declined.

'I'm really sorry it's ended this way,' he told her. 'I knew I'd found the girl of my dreams.'

'Can I ask you one thing before I go?'

'Go ahead.'

'What kind of business are you in?'

'The security business,' he answered blandly.

'What does that mean?'

'I offer a range of protective services. Why do you ask?'

'I'm just interested.'

She was picking up her satchel when the buzzer went.

'Police,' the voice said. 'We need to talk with you.'

'I've got unexpected visitors,' Duffy told Moira. 'Go into the kitchen while I'll deal with them.'

The detective was accompanied by a constable and Duffy invited them to sit down.

'A man called George Hagan was attacked with a sword in a betting shop in Maryhill three days ago and as a result of losing three fingers, could have bled to death.'

'What has it got to do with me?' he asked.

'You were there and ordered the sword to be used.'

'I don't know anything about this incident.'

'The owner of the shop tells us you were extorting money from him in a protection racket,' the detective disclosed. 'We want you down to the station for questioning.'

'I'd better let my girlfriend know,' he said.

But he went into his bedroom and transferred the gun from the bedside cabinet to his pocket before going into the kitchen and asking Moira to come through to the lounge.

'Change of plan,' he informed the detective. 'We're not going down to the station. We're walking out of here.'

'Don't be stupid, Duffy.'

He showed them the gun he had at Moira's back as he walked her towards the door.

'Press the button for the lift,' he ordered her.

Instead she turned and swung at him with her bag and the gun went off.

It was the first time that Marsaili had worn black since coming to university. Blue was her colour; the blue of the bay beyond the windows of her island home, a town in which there were no guns, no crooks. This was the reality of the city in which she was a student. People were being maimed or murdered while she stood in the vet school, cradling a small mammal in her arms. For many nights thereafter she wished her room in the Hall were full of smoke.

14. Getting the Picture

The young man who came off the afternoon train from the west coast practically fell through the door of Doig the bakers because of the army kitbag he had slung on his back, as well as the heavy case in his hand.

'Who's Mary Ann?' he asked breathlessly.

'I am,' the manageress confirmed as she came round the counter. 'Who are you?'

'Donald Macfarlane. My mother said I was to be sure and call in to see Mary Ann Mackinnon at the bakers because she would keep me right.'

'Who's your mother?' Mary Ann asked.

'Annie.'

'I hope she's well. What on earth have you got in that kitbag? You've not come down to join the army, have you?'

'No, no. It's *Practical Wireless*.'

'What's *Practical Wireless*?' the manageress requested enlightenment from the small youth who had a bad case of facial acne and whose ears were too prominent.

'It's a magazine I've been collecting since I was twelve.'

'You'd better sit down and have a cup of sweet tea and something to eat. Will you have fish or a meat pie?'

'It's not herring, is it?' the new arrival asked anxiously.

'What have you got against herring?' Mary Ann demanded to know, her fists on her hips. 'It kept many a poor soul alive on the island in the time of the famine, when people were dying of starvation in ditches. It's haddock, actually – fresh haddock from the east coast, because I wouldn't have frozen fish in this shop. How do you want your haddock done? In breadcrumbs, fried, or simmered in milk?'

'I'll take it fried.'

The manageress went through to the kitchen to place the order – including a portion of chips – with the cook, before going back through to hear the young man's reason for coming to Glasgow, laden down with *Practical Wireless* magazines.

Donald was an only child, a late baby delivered when his mother was forty two. When he was taken to the primary school with his satchel squint on his back he didn't have a word of English and Miss MacIsaac found great difficulty in instilling in him the basic principles of that language. She showed him a picture of a cow in a book and asked him to describe it.

'He's a cow.'

'No, Donald,' she said with infinite patience. 'That's not the way you say it. It's a cow, or that's a cow.'

The small boy looked at her uncomprehendingly.

'And what is this?' she asked, pointing to a picture of a tractor.

'He's a tractor.'

'No, Donald. *It's* a tractor.'

'Why?' the boy asked.

The teacher sighed, knowing that she couldn't get into a discussion on gender with this backward pupil whom she had decided to refer to the educational psychologist who came to the island every six months and conducted tests on children from families who had mental problems. In tests in which he was asked to fit simple shapes of wood together the boy scored highly. It was recalled that Donald's maternal grandfather had been a strange man who wouldn't open his own door to callers.

'What will I do with him?' his teacher appealed to the psychologist before he boarded the steamer for the mainland.

'I suggest you get him a set of building blocks.'

But she persevered and at the age of eight he finally mastered the art of reading. In his first year in secondary school he discovered an old set of *Practical Wireless* in the school library and became fascinated by the medium. Every evening his parents listened to the Gaelic news on their pre-war wireless which was powered by an accumulator, since the electricity supply hadn't reached their croft. Donald took off the back of the set and removed the valves and other parts, but mixed them up so much that he didn't know what went back where. His mother was in tears and his father had to take the parts down in a bag to Alex, the local radio dealer. He was charged fifteen shillings for having the Gaelic service restored.

But this experience didn't put Donald off. He pestered Mackay the technical teacher to help him build a crystal set.

'You realise, of course, that technically radios have become much more complex since these days,' the science teacher advised him.

'In what way, sir?'

Mackay went through to his office and brought back an object which he placed on the bench in front of the boy.

'Do you know what this is, Donald?'

'No, sir,' he said earnestly, staring at the pink plastic case.

'It's a transistor radio. It works with tiny parts. Switch it on.'

'How, sir?'

The science master showed him and the Beatles rocked the room.

'The tone is much clearer that one could ever get from crystal wirelesses.'

'How does it work, sir?' Donald asked, touching the plastic case as though it were a religious relic.

'It's quite complicated, Donald. You need some basic physics and maths.'

But though Donald didn't have this, he was still determined to pursue his dream of building a wireless receiver and eventually the science master relented and the class gathered round the bench to take turns listening with the earphones to the faint voice giving a commentary on a football match in Glasgow. Donald's father worked even harder to buy his son an annual subscription to *Practical Wireless*, which the boy kept on a specially installed shelf by his bed. He studied the diagrams in them by the light of the paraffin lamp, trying to follow the circuitry.

When it was time for him to leave school, because there was no prospect of him continuing further, since he had never passed an exam in his life, the headmaster called him into his office.

'What do you want to do with your life, Donald?'

'Work with radios.'

'You mean repairing them?'

'Yes sir.'

'But you don't have any qualifications in science,' the headmaster reminded the meek pupil who sat opposite him, his acne worsening by the week.

'But I understand what's going on inside a radio,' he maintained.

'I don't think we can get you into a technical college in Glasgow, but we might be able to get you an apprenticeship with a firm that repairs radios. They're also very likely to repair television sets, Donald, because this is the age of the television. New ones are coming off the boat every week for the island. In fact we hope to get one installed in the school next term – if we can get a decent signal.'

Donald had seen television sets in the houses of friends he had visited, but his first love was radio. The headmaster asked the science master to find out the names of companies in Glasgow which repaired radios and then the headmaster wrote to three of the firms, explaining that he had a 'school leaver who is fascinated by radio and television and who would like to work in the repair industry.'

'So you managed to get an apprenticeship,' Mary Ann re-iterated as she watched the youth consuming the fish and chips, over which he had shaken a quarter bottle of vinegar.

'I'm starting tomorrow with a company called St Mungo Rentals and Repairs.'

'Have you a place to stay?'

'I'm staying with a cousin of my mother's in Maryhill.'

'Is it a Gaelic speaking household?' the manageress wanted to know.

'I never asked.'

'I hope so. It's very important that you keep up your Gaelic in Glasgow. Too many people who come here deliberately lose the language because they don't want to be thought of as backward, but it's very useful to have here. I wouldn't have you sitting here, eating haddock and chips – followed by apple pie and custard – if you didn't speak the language. I'll take you to the Highlanders' Institute one night when there's a function on so that you can meet folk of your own age. Do you know how to get to your lodgings?'

He shook his head, so Mary Ann went to the drawer in her tiny office where she kept a booklet-style map of Glasgow, together with a bus timetable. She sat like a scholar working out the route and the number of bus he should take on an order slip, then tore it from its pad and handed it to him.

'If you get into any kind of bother, or if you feel depressed, come and see me,' was her parting valediction.

'How much?' he asked.

'How much what, Donald?'

'How much is the food?'

'The food is on me, a way of welcoming you to Glasgow,' she told him.

But the new arrival climbed on to the wrong bus and was

carried out to the suburbs. It took two hours and three transfers to take him to the tenement in Maryhill Road where he was greeted by his mother's elderly cousin Peigi, whose husband worked in a city slaughterhouse. He was given a room to himself but that night, lying in bed, listening to the traffic on the street below, he suffered homesickness as a physical sensation. The following morning when he reported to the works of St Mungo Rentals and Repairs, he lugged in the kitbag of *Practical Wireless* issues, almost knocking a young woman off the step of the bus as he struggled off with his burden, her handbag bursting open, having to pursue her lipstick tube along the gutter.

'Why have you brought in these magazines?' Tommy the supervisor asked.

'Because they've got a lot of interesting diagrams in them.'

'Dump them.'

'Dump them?' Donald repeated, shocked.

'Aye, because they're no use to you here. You're starting a five year apprenticeship and you'll go to night school. This business was set up to repair radios, but more and more people are buying television sets, which we supply on rental and therefore have to service. We've got ten engineers out in vans, doing just that.'

The new apprentice was given a brown overall and a place at a bench beside a morose engineer called Andy.

'You know what that is?' he asked, handing an object to Donald.

'A valve.'

'It's a valve all right, but there are different types of valves, and you're going to have to recognise them.'

Handing it back, Donald's elbow banged the bench and the valve exploded on the concrete floor at his feet.

'Now that was very clumsy of you,' Andy sighed, aware that he had been assigned a duffer. 'Valves cost money. Go and get a brush and shovel and sweep it up.'

Once a week the new apprentice went to night school to learn about the theory of radio and television transmission, but found it difficult following the diagrams on the blackboard, and when the tutor came round and looked at his exercise book, he asked the student if it were a knitting pattern he was drawing. Some evenings Donald ventured out into the city, wandering up Sauchiehall Street, looking into the window of a shop that sold radios and televisions. He marvelled at how small radio sets were becoming and he stood, sometimes in the rain, watching the picture on a television set, wishing he fully understood what lay behind the screen. He hadn't followed the supervisor's advice and dumped the issues of *Practical Wireless*. Lying in his lumpy bed in the dingy room with its askew blind, he studied the diagrams by the weak bulb, as if they contained a secret cipher which he would ultimately crack.

'You'll go out with one of the engineers, to see what they do,' the supervisor informed him one morning.

Donald sat beside Hector in the red van. He was the oldest employee in the firm and would retire in a year's time. He was respected for his ability to restore sound and vision to radios and televisions that seemed to be irreparable. But he had become lazy as he approached retirement and he said to Donald: 'You take this call.'

'Me?'

'Aye, go up and see what's wrang wi' the set and see if ye can pit it right. It's guid practice.'

The van was parked outside a smart block of flats on the south side of the city.

Donald took the tool case out of the back and pressed the silver button beside the customer's name on the plate by the door.

'Who is it?' a disembodied voice came weakly through the grille.

'Television repair,' Donald answered proudly.

'Push the door after you hear the buzzer,' the voice instructed. 'I'm on the third floor.'

He found himself in a marble-lined hall, seeing his own reflection in the steel doors of the elevator. He felt he looked the part, with the case, but he had never used a lift before, and tried to prise open the door with his fingers. When they wouldn't yield he took a screwdriver out of his case and was endeavouring to insert it between the doors when a man in golfing gear came out of a door.

'What on earth are you doing?' he demanded.

'Trying to open the doors.'

The man leaned across, pressed a button and the doors slid open.

'Who are you?' the man asked suspiciously.

'The television repair man,' Donald told him proudly.

'And where are you going in this building?'

'To Mrs Thomson's.'

The golfer wondered if he should let this strange looking

fellow ascend to the apartment where the elderly widow lived, alone, with valuable antiques, but he was late for his golfing round.

'Press that button,' he indicated, reaching into the elevator.

As the doors closed and the metal box began to rise Donald began to feel terror. Travelling to and from the mainland on the steamer that served the island, he was usually sick, even on relatively calm days, and had the lift not jolted to a halt, he would have left his breakfast on the floor.

Mrs Thomson led him into her elegant lounge, with its balcony and view of a well-tended garden.

'The picture suddenly went last night when I was watching The White Heather Club,' she explained. 'Dixie Ingram was about to do a Highland Fling and I was so irritated to miss him.'

Donald knelt on the carpet and sprang the catch of Hector's case. Everything required for a home repair was laid out in compartments, from valves to a soldering bolt, its cable coiled neatly and beside it, a small card with the silver flux wound round it.

The substitute repair man lifted a screwdriver from behind its retaining cord and unscrewed the back of the set. Then he tried to switch it on. All the valves were lit. He knew that he should have gone downstairs to fetch Hector, but he didn't want to appear ignorant in front of the customer, who was watching him, so he pushed the screwdriver into the works as if that would restore the picture.

The flash sent the elderly woman staggering against a

chair. Smoke was pouring from the set.

'Fire! Fire!' she was shouting.

'Open the window!' the repair man yelled.

She fumbled with the catch in the choking atmosphere as Donald used all his strength to lift the set from the floor. He yanked out the plug and staggered with his burden across the room, dropping it over the balcony. The crash was a cold frame disintegrating, as well as the screen smashing.

'My plants! My plants!' the customer was sobbing. 'I nurtured them so carefully, as if they were my babies.'

Donald rushed out of the flat and on to the landing. Instead of taking the lift, which was too complicated, he ran down the stairs and out to the van to tell Hector what had happened.

'Christ, ah should never huve trusted ye. Everyone in the works says you're a fool,' the technician said, forehead pressed to the steering-wheel.

A neighbour had come in to comfort Mrs Thomson at the loss of her set and tender plants. Having assured her that he would be back with a brand-new set that afternoon, at no extra charge, Hector went down to the garden to lift the wrecked set from the smashed cold frame and carried it out to the vehicle.

'Ye'll no' say a word about this to anyone or ah'll have ye oot of the works like that,' Hector threatened, snapping his fingers. 'Ye never went near that television, understood?'

When they returned to the works the supervisor asked Donald how he had fared on his first experience of a call.

'He wis very helpful,' Hector answered for him.

'Did you understand what Hector was doin' tae the set?' the supervisor enquired.

Donald looked at Hector and nodded.

'We were very lucky the customer's hoose didnae go on fire,' Hector said. 'The set short-circuited and ah had to throw it into her gerden.'

'Good thinking,' the supervisor complimented him. 'You were with a professional, Donald.'

That night in his dingy room, with the back issues of *Practical Wireless* stuffed in his father's kitbag hanging behind the door, the apprentice experienced his worst bout of depression since he had arrived in the city. The following day was Saturday, his day off, and he went to the bakery to see Mary Ann. The shop was very busy, but she always made time for people from her island, and she brought across a pot of tea for two and a cream horn to a vacant table of the eating area.

'What's the matter?' she began gently, having counselled depressed and inadequate islanders before.

'I'm not doing very well at the work.'

'But you haven't been there long, so it's bound to be strange. And you're in a strange city. Give yourself time to settle in.'

He recounted the shameful episode of the smoking television set.

'The technician you were out with should never have sent you up to do the job by yourself,' she told the wireless enthusiast, whose acne had flared violently after the trauma of Mrs Thomson's set. 'Put it down to part of the learning process.' She leaned forward confidentially. 'On the day I started here as a shop assistant I left a dozen pies under the grill and they went black and filled the place with smoke. They were for the Jesuits up in Garnethill, an order they'd been getting for years, but instead of giving me hell Father Dooley, who came to collect them, said: "They look like an order for the devil. Never mind, Mary Ann, accidents will happen," and he made the sign of the cross over my head. It almost made me want to become a Catholic.' She patted Donald's hand. 'So you go back and keep calm and listen and learn. It all takes time.'

The supervisor told Donald that he wanted him to learn to drive.

'It's essential if you're going out on the road. We'll pay for the lessons.'

The apprentice was terrified the first time he sat behind the wheel of the car. They were in a quiet part of the city, and he went so slowly – at twenty miles an hour – that a bus and half a dozen cars began blasting their horns behind him.

'A hearse goes faster than this,' the instructor rebuked him. 'Get up to thirty.'

On his second lesson Donald trod on the accelerator instead of the brake and ran into a bollard, damaging the wing of the car.

'You're going to have to pay a lot more attention,' the learner was told angrily.

Two months later and a failed test behind him, Donald was told by the supervisor that he was going out on the road with Keith, another technician, to gain further experience. Hector didn't tell his colleague that he had a dangerous man sitting beside him, and when they arrived at the house on the south side Keith said, 'I had one too many in the pub last night. I'm going for a snooze. You can go to the house and come back and tell me what's wrong with the set.'

Donald took the tool box out of the back of the van and opened the gate of the bungalow. He rang the bell and a woman's voice called: 'Let yourself in!' so he opened the glass door into the hall.

'I'll be through in a minute!' the same voice called. 'The set's in the lounge, on your left.'

Donald went in and switched it on. The screen was filled with wavy lines and he concluded that it was something to do with the aerial. The door opened behind him and the customer was standing behind him. She was wearing a diaphanous nightie and no dressing gown, and the way she was standing against the light, Donald saw everything.

'Smoke?' she asked, bending down to a table and holding out a packet of cigarettes to Donald.

He shook his head.

'I'm bored,' she announced, stretching her arms about her head so that the nightie hung on her nipples like a tempting curtain. 'My husband's away at sea for months.'

'I need to get a tool out of the van,' Donald told her in a trembling voice as he made for the door.

As Donald yanked open the driver's door of the van, the slumbering technician wakened with a start, banging his head on the roof.

'What the hell's happened?' he demanded.

'The woman's got hardly any clothes on,' the apprentice blurted out.

'You wait in the van for me and I'll attend to this job,' his

224

colleague said and didn't return for half an hour.

'What was wrong with the set?' Donald was curious to know when he returned.

'The set? Nothing. Just the adjustment of a knob.'

Donald is sitting his third driving test, the previous two having involved near collisions. He has already made an error in failing to indicate turning to his left and he says a mild Gaelic expletive in his frustration.

'What did you say?' the instructor wants to know.

His examinee apologises.

'You spoke in Gaelic. Where do you come from?'

Donald names the island.

'I'm from there too,' the man tells him in Gaelic. 'Where about on the island?'

When Donald names the town, he's asked about his family, and it turns out that the examiner knows his father. The test resumes.

'Stop!' the examiner shouts.

It takes Donald vital seconds to respond to the emergency call, but at the end of the test the examiner writes him a pass slip and wishes him 'all the best' in Gaelic. 'Tell your father that Dougie MacCorquodale asked kindly after him.'

Several months after passing his test Donald is told that he'll have to go out on repairs by himself, because four of the technicians are off with 'flu. He gets behind the wheel of the red van and sets out, a map of the city on the seat beside him, beside a list of his calls. He's supposed to complete fifteen calls in a day, but Donald wasn't good at geography at school and once failed to point out Glasgow on the map slung across the blackboard. He ends up having to wind down the window to ask four separate pedestrians for directions and even then he gets lost again. Eventually, after an hour and a half, he arrives at his first call, in a housing scheme notorious for its crime. The man who opens the door to him has a shaven head and is wearing braces over his bare shoulders and ex-army boots laced tight round the ankles.

'Ah canna get the fuckin' fitba,' the man tells the technician.

Donald wants to ask for a translation, but is terrified in this malodorous house which has a dartboard affixed to one wall, the paper around it pockmarked, where the missile went off-course. He unscrews the back of the set, pretends to examine the innards, then announces that he'll have to take it to the workshop.

'When will ah get it back?' the man asked aggressively. 'There's a big match on the night.'

Donald says he'll try to return with it in the late afternoon, though he knows that's an unrealistic estimate. He wants out of this place as soon as possible, especially since a vicious looking dog with splayed paws has appeared and is snarling at him. He staggers out with the set, almost losing his footing on the bare concrete stairs, and slides it into the back of the van. After four calls – the number he manages for the day – there are four sets in the back of the van.

'Why have you brought them all back?' the supervisor asks in frustration. 'You're supposed to repair them on-site. Tomorrow I want twelve calls and not more than two sets brought here because the boys on the benches can't cope.'

The following clear morning Donald sets out, with the

map and call-list on the seat beside him. He has at last dumped the back issues of *Practical Wireless* and is using the kitbag to carry his thermos of tea and the pieces that his landlady has made up for his lunch. His first call is to a semi-detached villa in Jordanhill where he is asked to wipe his shoes on the hessian mat before stepping onto the fitted-carpet. The television set is in a bay-windowed lounge overlooking a private garden, the grass rimed with frost. The lady of the house brings a sheet of brown paper for the repair man to set his case down on, to save the carpet from being sullied. Having established that there's no picture, Donald unscrews the back. He uses leads to test the power and sees that a valve needs replacing. The woman is pleased with her restored picture and gives him a ten shilling note. On the way out, the corner of his case knocks a stand, and the Chinese vase displayed on it falls to the carpet and shatters. The householder puts her ringed fingers to her made-up face and begins to scream, as though she's being assaulted. Donald is trying to say sorry but she shoves him out of the door and turns the key before getting down on her knees to lift the fragments of the irreparable object.

Donald has lost his nerve early in the day and by lunch-time, when he's consuming his piece in a quiet street, a football bouncing against the windscreen of the van, there are two sets in the back. By three o' clock this has increased to four. Donald decides not to make any further calls, though this is only a quarter of his daily quota. The brief winter day is darkening and the headlights of homeward-bound commuters are dazzling him as he drives, hunched over the wheel. What's he going to do? He knows that if he takes four sets into the repair shop he'll be sacked. His face is on fire with acne and, as usual, he's lost. He can't stop to consult the map because he's in a traffic queue and already horns at his rear have warned him about going too slow.

Without indicating and with a protesting horn pressed down by the heel of the driver's hand behind him, the red van turns into a street. Donald doesn't know where he is and he doesn't care. He's so exhausted that he falls asleep, leaning back in the seat, his mouth wide open. A woman on her way to bingo sees him in the lighted interior and bangs on the door.

'Are ye a' right in there, son?'

There seems to be no name on the street. Donald drives on, past lighted windows and illuminated signs advertising dancing and alcoholic drinks. Ahead of him he sees the profiles of cranes, like prehistoric monsters rearing against the skyline. He has arrived at the river. He has an idea and brakes so suddenly that the vehicle behind him stops inches from his bumper and as she passes him, the female driver behind the wheel of the Mercedes lowers her window and gives him two fingers.

Donald opens the back of the van, lifts the first television set on to the parapet and hears the splash. The other three follow. Donald is now in familiar territory and before he parks his van in Maryhill he bursts the lock on the back door.

'Did you have a busy day?' his landlady asks as she serves him haddock from a blackened pan.

'Very busy.'

The following morning he reports that he had four sets

in the back of his van for major repairs, having examined them thoroughly on-site, but that the lock on the back door of his van was forced overnight in Maryhill and the sets stolen.

'At least we're covered by the insurance,' the exasperated supervisor says. 'You'll work at the bench from now on.'

On the bus home, Donald finds an evening paper on the seat.

CLYDE MYSTERY

An elderly woman whose flat overlooks the Clyde phoned the police last night to report that she saw what she believed to be four bodies being pushed over the parapet of Stockwell Bridge into the river. She noticed a vehicle parked on the bridge. Police are sending a diver down today to investigate.

15. Scotia Street

The tall imposing man who descended from the steam train in Buchanan Street Station looked like an undertaker accompanying a coffin in the guard's van. Archie Maclean was wearing a long black coat and a black homburg with a wide brim – his 'funeral attire,' as his wife Alice called it, as she brushed the headgear before the bank manager walked up the brae to see one of his customers laid to rest. The only time he condescended to leave the island – apart from a day's excursion to the nearest town on the mainland to buy a suit – was when he went to Glasgow in the autumn for the annual dinner of the bank. Their son and daughter have qualified in medicine and veterinary science and are beginning their careers, both of them in Glasgow. The patriarch made an exception and attended their graduations. The engagement party for Murdo and his sweetheart Una was held on her home island of Islay, with a bonfire of driftwood on the shore of Loch Indaal and music and dancing. Alice thoroughly approves of her son's choice. Marsaili's romance with Roderick MacKenze didn't last, despite their mutual interest in Gaelic and she's at present unattached.

This is the early 1970s and Alice refuses to make concessions to fashion. She sees no need to dispose of a wardrobe that has served her well and attracted compliments in her years as the wife of the bank manager, helping to run whist drives to raise funds for the blind, or serving cold lunches to the judges in a dim tent at the island's Highland Games. Alice has a love affair with the colour red and today she is wearing a red hat with a brim as wide as her husband's, who is walking beside her, carrying the same case with the reinforced corners which he carried to this same city when he came here in the mid 1930s to learn the skills of banking.

'I had Mrs Mackinnon in the office yesterday and I promised her we would call on Mary Ann,' the banker informs his wife as he stops outside Doig's.

'I'm looking for Mary Ann Mackinnon,' the bank manager tells the young woman behind the counter.

'You've found her,' she says with a smile.

Later, in their hotel room, the banker and his spouse will continue to wonder at the transformation of the bakery manageress from the oversized creature they watched waddling along Main Street, to the slim elegance of the person now greeting them in effusive Gaelic from behind the counter.

'You'll have a meal,' Mary Ann insists. She has a pale, ethereal colour to her complexion because she still cries herself to sleep at the loss of her lover the piper, who took off a while before. No one else has been invited to supper, or into her double bed, which seems cold and too large now.

'No thank you, Mary Ann, we're going to the bank dinner tonight,' Alice tells her.

'But you won't have eaten on the train.'

'We had sandwiches and a flask,' Alice informs her.

'If you won't have lunch you'll have tea' Mary Ann insists.

While the afternoon tea is being laid out on plates by one of her assistants the manageress slides on to the padded bench opposite the new arrivals. She and Archie talk in Gaelic, a conversation from which his wife is excluded because grandparents failed to pass on the language, believing that it had no value. While Archie conveys greetings from Mary Ann's parents, including the caution that she must keep well wrapped up in the cold autumnal spell which covers their croft on the island with frost, Alice looks around and concludes that the shop could do with a good clean.

The afternoon tea arrives on a large tray slid on to the table – sandwiches cut into triangles for these arrivals of consequence from the island, a stand of cakes, including scones and cream horns and a large silver-plated pot of tea with a matching jug of hot water. Mary Ann distributes the china and knives. Alice eats sparingly, the consequence of having to feed first two sons and two daughters before she can sit down to the leftovers. She is one of those persons who will nibble all day, at bits of biscuit, a slice of toast. The scone she is offered is city-sized and after she has sliced it in two she returns half to the stand.

After half an hour, in which the bank manager has given the exile an account of births, marriages and deaths on the island in the past months, Alice announces that they must make for their hotel. The banker holds Mary Ann by the shoulders and kisses her on the cheek.

'She's kindly,' he remarks when they're out on Buchanan Street.

'Yes, at giving away what isn't hers and which we didn't want anyway,' his wife reminds him.

Archie is smiling. This shrewd man realises that the owners of the bakers are subsidising new arrivals to the city from the island, but this does not concern him unduly because the manageress is performing an important function in welcoming islanders and putting them at ease in the unfamiliar city by talking to them in Gaelic and feeding them. They know that if they have problems – if they want to change their lodgings, or feel the need to converse in Gaelic – they need only pay Doig's a visit. The banker knows that in that trim bosom, Mary Ann has a large heart.

The banker and his wife always stay in the St Enoch Hotel in the Square of that name, because that is where the bank dinner is held. Archie likes this building because it represents the architectural grandeur that Glasgow is losing as buildings are demolished to make way for ugly offices and lethal roads. The two arrivals follow the silent shoes of the porter with their case into the lift and up to their floor, where their room overlooks the Square below. The black coat and homburg are shed and Archie stands at the window in his waistcoat with a cigarette. He's remembering the day when he was called into the manager's office in the west coast branch and told that he was being transferred to Glasgow 'to give you experience, Maclean,' the manager says. He's one of the old-fashioned breed who wears a wing collar, with a stick pin (with the Masonic emblem of compasses) in his sober tie, and with a heavy gold watch chain crossing his waistcoat. His bowler hat is on the stand to the left of his desk.

'You will, of course, have to find your own accommodation, Maclean.'

That day in the mid-1930s when he descended from the steam train with the new case which he had bought at the saddlers (who embossed his initials in black in a bottom corner for an extra two shillings), Mary Ann Mackinnon had still to be born, and the manageress of Doig's of that era (glimpsed through the window by the new arrival) was wearing a puffed-up white cap as a concession to hygiene. But Archie Maclean walked on. He knew where he was going, but he didn't know how to get there, so he stopped to ask a policeman.

'Scotia Street? That's off New City Road,' the constable confirmed the location, then told him which tram to take.

Archie Maclean sat in the sparking machine which was swaying so much that it seemed at any moment it would topple from the rails and crush the cart and horse that was pacing it, the horse blinkered, its large feathered hooves lifted high, pounding the cobbles, the driver with a cigarette in the corner of his mouth, his cap on back to front.

At first Archie thought that the suitcase between his feet was being stolen, but the conductress had kicked it.

'Get it oot o' ma way!' she warned him. 'See if ah break an ankle –' The machine spat the ticket at the frightened traveller. He was going to have asked the conductress to tell him where to get off, but he appealed to the elderly man sitting beside him instead and was given what amounted to a lecture on the topography of the city that made him fear he would be carried far beyond his destination, out into the suburbs.

'This is New City Road, son!'

The young banker descends into the bustle of the city, past a shop where fish lie, mouths open as if surprised at ending up on ice on a marble slab. Archie Maclean will eat many of them – notably mackerel – during his sojourn in Glasgow. He notices men lounging at street corners. He's arrived in Glasgow in the Depression. Some of these men have been building ships that now stand uncompleted on stocks in river yards until better times come. Some of them are wide boys who shun employment and make their money resetting stolen goods. Others are plain idle.

Archie will have to get used to the noise and activity – the busy pavements, the vehicles driven down Great Western Road and along New City Road, into the city. He sees a long sleek car that left the west coast early that morning. The hood is down and it's being driven by a man wearing a deerstalker in which salmon flies are embedded. His spouse or mistress beside him is wearing a fetching jockey cap.

The young banker turns into Scotia Street and locates the number. His shoes echo in the grimy tiled close and up the worn steps to the second landing where he lifts the brass knocker in the shape of a hand, a welcoming signal. A shadow approaches towards the engraved glass door and when he has identified himself a safety chain is disengaged.

'*Fàilte gu Glaschu!*' the elderly woman welcomes him.

Archie doesn't reply because, though his parents spoke Gaelic, they used it in the household as a confidential means of communication so that their children wouldn't know what was being said.

'You don't speak Gaelic and you from the west coast,' the elderly woman says in wonder and sorrow. 'We'll have to do something about that.'

Archie Maclean steps into the residence of Mrs Annie Macinnes, his mother's sister-in-law, and into what will become some of the happiest years of his life. She's a widow, having lost her husband in the horror of the Great War. Archie is shown into the bedroom – the only one in the flat – which he's to share with another young man who is presently at work, a rarity in that depressed city. Annie sleeps in the kitchen, in a discreetly curtained-off bed in the recess. Archie will call her the *cailleach* (old woman), but not to her face, because there seems such a distance between their ages, though she isn't yet seventy.

'This is the sitting-room,' she tells her new resident, opening a door.

He sees a daybed in brown moquette, a piano and some kind of plant before the door is closed again.

There wasn't the luxury of a bathroom in the flat. Mrs Macinnes explained that in the morning she would vacate the kitchen early, so that her two lodgers could wash and shave at the sink before going to their places of business. The toilet on the landing was shared between all the flats in the building. But Archie wasn't disappointed: these were the conditions which prevailed in many houses on the west coast, where the heather moorland was the toilet and where, unlike Scotia Street, there was no switch to snap on the light. He would come to love this basic late Victorian billet like his own home and his landlady would be like a mother to him.

Maclay Days

At six o' clock his fellow lodger came in. He was a tram driver, a useful bedfellow to have for a new arrival to the city. His name was Peter MacCuish and he came from the island where Archie would later be bank manager and where he would perfect the Gaelic he had acquired in Scotia Street. The tram driver was a Gaelic speaker and on that first night in his new lodgings, Archie Maclean was informed by his landlady that there were to be no concessions.

'Gaelic is the language of this household and it will continue to be, not out of discourtesy to you, but because the only way you are going to learn the language is if you hear it spoken and then speak it yourself. When I feel you need it I'll give you an English translation.'

As the two lodgers sat opposite each other at the kitchen table, eating mackerel and potatoes, Annie bustled about, talking in Gaelic to the tram driver. At first Archie would be confused and would despair of ever becoming proficient in the language, but soon he would begin to realise that, having heard Gaelic at home since childhood, he had known instinctively from the expressions on his parents' faces what they were talking about and he also found that somehow he had learned the pronunciation without assimilating the sense.

The following morning, on Peter's instructions, Archie took the number 13 red tram to the bank in St Vincent Place. In the coming years he would enjoy this journey into work, sitting with familiar faces in the tram, on mornings of rain and sunshine. Like many young men of that generation he wore a soft hat with a snappy brim and a light-coloured overcoat with a half-belt at the back, garb copied from American screen idols. His shoes were always polished and his landlady kept a crease in the trousers of his business suit with an iron heated on the coal-fired range.

The bank in the centre of the city was an imposing place with a cavernous entrance, marble floors and mahogany counters, behind one of which Archie Maclean stood, depositing and dispensing money mostly for businessmen who brought in their takings in leather bags with padlocks. Archie wore a red rubber pad with nodules on a finger, which allowed him to count a batch of notes at such speed, it appeared that he was demonstrating a conjuring trick.

The bank's business was done for the day before the rush hour and Archie took the same number of tram back to Scotia Street. Before having his supper with Peter, he would have a conversational class in Gaelic with his landlady. He had bought a Gaelic grammar which he studied on the tram to and from work, finding that his grasp of the language was growing daily with his immersion in the conversation of Scotia Street. In later years, when he was a bank manager, he would have profound moments of nostalgia for Scotia Street and its environs. Though he was breathing in the pure air blown across the Atlantic as he stood on the bank steps, conversing in Gaelic with a local, he would suddenly smell the reek of smoke from the chimneys of Scotia Street and would hear, in the sound of shoes hurrying along Main Street, the clatter of hooves on New City Road as a horse hauled a cart of fresh vegetables in from the country for the enjoyment of diners in the smart restaurants of the city centre.

He loved the varied society of Scotia Street. In the dawn he would hear a miner's boots on the stairs as he descended for a day to be spent in the darkness of underground when the sun was shining in the city. Shaving in the morning at the kitchen sink, with the window open, his razor, clicking against the side of the enamel cup that held the hot water, would keep time to the Italian tenor practising in the flat below. On summer mornings it would be a joyful aria, his voice soaring above the early traffic, mechanical and animal. In the next flat there was a chocolate maker and when that window was open, Archie could scent the confection cooking on the open range. There was a blacksmith several closes along, his smithy in another part of the city in which horses still held their own against motorised traffic. There was a public house in the street where Archie and his bedfellow enjoyed a dram on a Friday night. If he had a hangover, he could descend in the early hours and buy a pint bottle of fresh milk at the dairy, and the chemist could provide a powder for a sore head. There was a gas lamplighter, since parts of the city still weren't switched on. If he were hungry he could buy a meat pie in Simple Simon the bakers in New City Road and if he were short of money until pay day, he could take his wrist watch round to the pawnbrokers in that same road.

On Sunday morning he accompanied his landlady to St Columba Gaelic Church because, she said, there was no better way to master the language of Eden than by studying the Bible. In the beginning, much of the minister's soaring rhetoric was lost on the young bank teller, but in the fullness of time he came to understand the dire warnings directed at those who fell by the wayside. On winter evenings there was a ceilidh round the banked-up grate in the kitchen in Scotia Street. Mrs Macinnes kept a pot of broth heated for callers from the west. Her daughter Christine, known as Neenie, was married to a policeman called Willie MacColl. Neenie was in her late thirties and pretty, with auburn hair and a preference for Fairisle jumpers. The MacColls lived practically round the corner in St Peter's Street and Willie would break off from his beat along New City Road to warm his hands at Annie's radiant coals and to accept a dram to heat his insides. When he apprehended someone for a misdemeanour, he had a simple question to ask: '*Co as a tha thu?*' ('where are you from?') and if they answered in Gaelic, he closed his notebook, restored it to his tunic pocket and told them to be more careful in the future.

The gathering in a tenement in Scotia Street was like a ceilidh in a *taigh dubh*, a black house, the only absences being the hens that seemed to be listening to the *sgeulachdan* as they roosted on the backs of chairs. As the level in the whisky bottle sank stories were told of people with *an dà sealladh*, the two sights, who saw the funerals of the still living passing, and encountered the dead on lonely roads. Archie listened to these stories, but he was too young, too eager for the experiences of life to be concerned about his destination after death, which seemed inconceivably far away.

'Is the city quiet tonight?' Neenie would ask her spouse after the supper of herring and potatoes had been served, not on plates (because they would have to be washed) but on a newspaper spread on the table, the feast eaten with the fingers, the skins and bones bundled up and put into the bin.

'There are a few keelies about.' All the words in the sentence, except *keelies*, were delivered in Gaelic, as if there were no word in the language to describe such a person. But Archie knew what he meant. Glasgow was plagued by gangs

Maclay Days

and one evening, returning from a visit to the city centre, he witnessed the meeting of the Cow Toi and the Milton Tongs in New City Road. From his grandstand view on the top deck of the stalled tram Archie saw faces being opened up by flicked razors and bicycle chains spun round heads. For a time it looked as if the warring gangs would topple the tram, but a posse of mounted police came clattering, laying about the heads and shoulders of the brawlers with big sticks. The gangs scattered down side streets, including Scotia Street, leaving the area round the tram stained with blood.

But Willie MacColl knew how to deal with keelies. Any aggression or show of a weapon and this policeman would put a headlock on the challenger. Yet, sitting at his mother-in-law's kitchen grate and sipping his dram, his talk was of the flowers and wildlife in the landscape of his home island before fitting on his hat to descend into the world of razor-wielding keelies again, his boots echoing up the closes of New City Road.

Archie Maclean always bought an evening paper before swinging on to the tram at the end of the day's business in the bank. He read the front page as he was jolted home from St Vincent Street to a supper of wholesome fare of fish or black puddings. It was clear that there was going to be a war and some evenings after supper he roamed the lighted band on Mrs Macinnes's wireless in the sitting-room, picking up the Führer delivering a speech. Though the bank teller didn't have German, it was evident from the ranting tone that seemed in danger of overheating the valves, that the dictator was planning war, and not only against the '*Juden*'.

Archie also used the sitting-room to write poetry. Though

it was light nostalgic verse extolling the beauties of his west coast home, it was published when he submitted it to the evening paper and a welcome cheque for a guinea would arrive which he would spend on a bottle of whisky for the kitchen ceilidh. He was now so proficient in Gaelic that he could maintain a conversation with Mrs Macinnes. It would become clear in the course of Archie's career, though he became a successful bank manager, that leafing through books and not piles of banknotes was his true profession. He should have been in the Celtic department of one of the universities, lecturing on the language and going out into the field to record songs and stories which were in danger of dying with those who had learned them at their mother's knee.

However, when the Empire Exhibition was staged in Glasgow in 1938 and a typical Highland clachan was erected on the site, Archie took his landlady by tram to visit it, to proudly show her one of his poems adorning a wall. It was in Gaelic, with an English translation, and Mrs Macinnes took a small pencil from her handbag and made a slight correction to the Gaelic text.

On the Sunday morning that war was declared, Archie Maclean should have been in St Columba Gaelic Church listening to a sermon. Instead he was sitting with Mrs Macinnes at her wireless, listening to Chamberlain's ominous announcement. The following day he came back from work to find Sarah Milton, a neighbour, sitting crying in Mrs Macinnes's kitchen.

'Her boy and girl are being evacuated to the country,' the landlady explained to her lodger. 'I'm telling Sarah that it's for their safety. Glasgow could be bombed.'

'But I'll miss them,' the inconsolable mother moaned.

The following afternoon children emerged from the closes of Scotia Street, carrying small cases, their names on labels round their necks. They were dressed in their Sunday best, cute bonnets, coats with velvet collars, buttoned shoes. After work Archie went to meet Mrs Macinnes and Neenie at Central Station. There were hundreds of children on the platform, many of them crying, some of them comforting their mothers at the parting. Archie was both shocked and distressed at this early emotional casualty of the war.

Among the customers in the bank in Archie's home town where he had worked before being transferred to Glasgow, a pretty dark-haired young woman came in every Friday afternoon with the takings of a dress shop on the seafront. As Archie counted the coins, sliding them off the polished counter into his palm, he made conversation with the customer. Her name was Alice and soon he was meeting her every weekday lunchtime and, weather permitting, taking her arm along the esplanade. Alice was always elegant because her employer used her as a model for garments and hats. On wet days they sat in a shelter in which Archie was permitted his first kiss. He had recently acquired a motor bike and some evenings appeared at her door to take her for a spin. Alice's mother was dubious at his ability to handle the large black throbbing machine, but he was a well mannered young man who lifted his hat to her when they met, so she let her daughter go with him.

Archie has come home from the city to see his sweetheart. He's changed his soft hat for a leather helmet and Alice was warned to leave her wide-brimmed headgear at home, otherwise it'll be carried away. She's wearing a polka dot dress which she's tucked in behind her shapely knees as the bike negotiates bends.

However, when he's transferred to Glasgow, Archie leaves his bike in the shed at home. One weekend a month he takes the Friday evening train north so that he can see his parents and sweetheart and on the weekend after war is declared he roars up to her house on his motor bike. He produces the ring which he bought in the Argyll Arcade in Glasgow and which will need a slight adjustment by a jeweller in the seaport to fit her finger. Her mother, a war widow, approves of the engagement. Later, Archie takes Alice into town on his bike and they have a coffee in a café on the seafront, where the rays of the sun sinking into the sea catch the solitaire on her finger.

'I think we should get married soon,' Archie announces.

'Why the hurry? We're only just engaged,' Alice points out, her spoon in the cup sounding like a little bell as she stirs in sugar.

'Because of the war.'

'What does that mean?' Alice presses him.

'I'll probably be called up.'

This prediction makes Alice shudder, as if a sudden cold breeze from the sea has swept through the café.

The thought that the man sitting opposite her, smoking a cigarette, could be drafted into the navy terrifies her and she has a vision of a destroyer, fatally wounded by a torpedo, going down, with her fiancé waving frantically from the tilting deck. If they marry soon she would be left a widow.

'We should fix a date for next year, the earlier the better,' he tells her.

'I'll have to talk to my mother,' she warns him.

'Of course. But I'd like you to come down to Glasgow before then.'

'What would I do?' she asks in surprise.

'You don't need to do anything. I have money saved.'

When Alice put this proposition to her mother, she was apprehensive, because she didn't want to lose the company of her only child. But at the end of the following month Alice gave her notice to the proprietor of the dress shop and in the spring of 1940 she was lodged with a pleasant woman in Shamrock Street, very near to Scotia Street, where she ate her supper with her future husband. In the evenings they walked in Kelvingrove Park, underneath the Park Circus mansions where, over twenty years later, their first child Murdo would reside in Maclay Hall as a medical student.

On the last night of his retirement pilgrimage to Glasgow Dr Murdo Maclean went along Elmbank Street to the original Highlanders' Institute, where exiles from the north and west had gathered before it moved to Berkeley Street in the early 1960s. When he located the number he discovered that the premises were a smart hotel. He went into the desk and asked the receptionist if there were any photographs of the building in its former use.

'We don't have anything like that, sir,' she informed him, looking at him as if she were speaking to an elderly man who was losing his memory and had wandered into the wrong building.

'This was the Highlanders' Institute up until the beginning of the nineteen sixties,' he insisted.

'I wasn't born until 1986, sir.'

She pressed a bell to summon help and a porter came through. When he too denied any knowledge of the history of the building Dr Maclean took him by the elbow to the door and showed him the word *Failte* carved on the woodwork above.

'Now you come to mention it, sir, someone said it had been a dance hall,' the porter recalled.

'Can I see the dance floor?' Murdo requested.

'There's no dance floor here, sir. It's all been filled in with bedrooms.'

'My parents were married here during the war,' Murdo told him. 'But the dance was disrupted.'

The Highlanders' Institute in Elmbank Street was booked for eighty on Thursday 13 March 1941, and the majority took the train from the west coast. It was crowded with solders and sailors returning from leave and some of the wedding guests had to stand in the corridors. The service was held in St Columba Gaelic Church. The groom was wearing a swallow-tailed coat and the bride a wedding dress of Belgian lace, the gift from Miss Maxton, her former employer. After the ceremony they walked the short distance to Elmbank Street, where they cut the cake for the photographers. The married couple led off with a waltz to a selection of Gaelic tunes.

Outside, a full moon shone on the serene city, as if hostilities had ceased and the world had returned to sanity. Alice would remember seeing it reflected in the mirror of the cloakroom as she fixed her mouth, after receiving so many kisses in congratulations. They would spend their honeymoon night in the Grand Hotel at Charing Cross and the next morning take a train for the north.

'We were about to dance an eightsome reel when the sirens went,' Alice recalled to her children as she smoked by the peaceful window overlooking the bay in the bank house on the island. Though it's a still summer evening, with the bay crowded with yachts, the cigarette at Alice's lips trembles. That moon of her wedding night was treacherous, because it allowed the Luftwaffe bombers to follow the silver thread of the river to the vital shipyards of Clydebank. The first bombs made the sugar couple on top of the wedding cake shudder and it seemed that the fluted pillars supporting the two tiers would collapse. Willie MacColl had to hurry home to St Peter's Street to put on his police uniform. The band stopped and the wedding guests stood fearfully, listening to the detonations.

'I was sure the city would be next,' Alice recalls to her offspring.

Two of the guests were nurses in the west coast hospital, and they went away in their wedding finery to see if they could be of assistance. The remainder of the wedding party were too fearful to brave the streets on the way back to their hotels and most of them would spend the night there, sprawled in chairs and curled up on sofas.

'There were bedrooms at the top of the Highlanders and we were given one,' Alice disclosed to her family. 'But who could have slept through that?'

Though she was too delicate to refer to her nuptials, it

wasn't possible to consummate their marriage when Clydebank was being pulverised, so they lay together, exhausting their supply of cigarettes as searchlights seeking out the invaders formed crosses in the sky. In the morning they shared the other tier of the wedding cake with their guests and went out into the city to hear about the appalling overnight blitz. Precious oil stocks had gone up in flames; schools and churches had been hit.

They could smell the carnage in the air. They had decided that they would forego their honeymoon and instead head home to the relative safety of the west coast. But first they went round to Scotia Street. Willie had come in an hour before, having been up all night at Clydebank. As he ate his breakfast he described how the incendiaries had lit up the targets and how tenement walls had collapsed, revealing rooms. In one first floor flat he had seen an old woman slumped in an armchair. She had obviously died of shock, but the body couldn't be reached because the stairs had gone.

'There must be hundreds dead,' Willie told the newly weds. 'When I left an hour ago people were piling what they could salvage into prams and carts.'

'We have one survivor here,' Neenie, who had stayed overnight with her terrified mother, announced. She went to the sideboard and removed a cloth to show a cage.

'What is it?' Alice asked, poking her finger through the bars to the little yellow bird huddled on the spar.

'It's a canary,' Willie said. 'A woman came up to me and said: "This is all I managed to take from my house. Will you hold the cage for me for ten minutes until I go and look for my sister?" Ten minutes after she left me there was another explosion and I assume she was killed.'

'I doubt this bird will ever sing again,' Neenie said sadly. 'I gave it some oatmeal but it's just sitting there.'

'I'll need to go for a sleep and get back to Clydebank,' Willie told them.

'We're going home on the evening train,' Archie said.

It was crowded and Alice, demure in a pillbox hat, was given a seat by a drunken sailor on leave from a battleship that would be sunk within the year. The train ran through the glens with its blinds down in case of attack because of its moving lights and when it was taking in water at a remote station, the passengers could see the southern sky light up as Clydebank was being hit for a second night.

'We're lucky not to be in the city,' Archie told his bride as they smoked on the platform.

But the drama of the evening wasn't over. A big man came lurching into their compartment, recognised Archie and almost lifted him out of his seat with his greeting. They had been in school together and in the same shinty team, where Norman Kennedy had cut a swathe through the opposition with his stick.

'Here's the hero,' Archie announced.

'The hero?' Alice asked, uneasy at the new arrival's overpowering presence, especially with his leg pressing against her thigh as he swayed above her with the train rattling beside a dark loch.

'This man escaped from the Germans,' Archie informed his bride.

The other soldiers who were sleeping in the compartment woke up.

'I wouldn't be here today if it wasn't for Gaelic,' Kennedy revealed. 'God bless the tongue I was born with, though I never thought it would have such value to me in life.'

The occupants of the carriage listened to the thrilling story. Kennedy had been with the Highland Division at the fall of France and for five days he and a few other men had held out in a château, the fine plasterwork of the salons wrecked by German shells, the family portraits sprayed with machine-gun fire.

'The German commander who accepted the surrender of the château said he was amazed at the small number of men that had been holding them off. We were marched to a field beyond Abbeveille and given a glass of cider. I was thinking: how am I going to escape? We were driven in lorries about twenty kilometres and met up with prisoners from other regiments, Camerons, Seaforths, Gordons, the Black Watch, and some French troops. And we also came across men from the Argylls. They had all been captured at St Valery, while trying to get away across the Channel. We only had some British Army biscuits to eat and two days later we were on the road again.'

The narrator paused to light a cigarette, using a bullet made into a lighter, a souvenir, he said, from his time in France. Alice was studying his face in the flame, deciding that he was handsome, but also ruthless looking. She was disconcerted by the size of his hands.

'Where was I? Ah yes. We were marched through St Pol and Bruay. And French women ran out to hand us bread and cigarettes. This is where I met up with a Corporal called

MacTaggart and I told him: "stuff your bread in your tunic and save it for later, because we won't be staying with this column for much longer." There was another chap I knew, Iain MacKnight, and when a woman came out with a pail of water for us, I said to the two of them: "now's our chance". We went behind her and into her garden.'

The epic tale continued in the swaying train, with every-one in the carriage listening to the narrator, who paused now and then to take a swig from a bottle of whisky. The fugitives had exchanged their uniforms for stolen civilian clothes and were fed in a house by a family whose patriarch had been a prisoner of the hated Germans during the last war.

'We reached the Canadian War Memorial at Vimy Ridge at about eight in the evening. Have you ever seen a photograph of it?' Kennedy asked Alice. 'It's the huge figure of a woman weeping for the fallen in the Great War, with her head bowed, a beautiful piece of work. I was admiring it against the sky when I fell asleep in a haystack. We were wakened by coughing sounds and discovered that there was a German cavalry camp across the way. We had to crawl through a field of corn on our hands and knees to get away. We came to a bridge with two sentries and decided that the only way was to march past them. They actually said "good morning" to us.'

The story became more and more thrilling to the occupants of the carriage, like a moving ceilidh house, the narrator's cigarette transcribing an arc in the darkness to illustrate his story: challenged by a Frenchwoman that they were English, but told that she wouldn't betray them to the Germans; and the following night, sheltering in a shed, another Frenchwoman entered. 'She said to us: "Do you know that the war's over? France has surrendered. I've just heard it on the wireless." She told us that she would help us to get back home if we could prove that we were British, so I produced a photograph of myself wearing the peace-time uniform of the Argylls. She was very taken with it. I think she quite fancied me.'

They were surprised in a barn in Cambrai by German soldiers who asked if they were refugees and when they confirmed this in their basic French they were told to sleep on. On their way to Amiens they picked up an invalid chair, filling it with tins of biscuits and fruit and two bottles of rum from a deserted café. Archie Maclean had read the story of their escape which had been featured in several newspapers, but knew that it had been highly censored, not only because it would deliver important information to the enemy, but also because of Kennedy's reputation. Archie had been told that he had been dismissed from the Glasgow Police for brutality against the razor-wielding gangs, permanently disabling some of them. He had also heard another version of Kennedy's story in Gaelic: sentries hadn't been passed with a polite good morning, but had been bayoneted by Kennedy, their pockets looted for cigarettes. One of the houses they had entered belonged to a priest. Kennedy had heard him on the phone and assumed that he was betraying them to the Germans, and had strangled him with the cord of the instrument he had been speaking into.

Was such brutality justified, Archie asked himself, recalling how the German raids had pulverised Clydebank the night before and had returned to inflict more punishment. But the narrator was reaching the climax of his story, the whisky bottle almost empty. They were taken prisoner and brought before the commandant of the camp, who pointed his revolver at each of them in turn.

'He asked us to state our nationality and I replied in Gaelic: "I don't know." When he asked me where we came from I told him "Ardnamurchan." A number of men were brought in to question us in Dutch, Spanish, German, Polish and Italian. Then an atlas was produced and we were asked to point to our country of origin as he took us through the various countries one by one. When he came to the Ukraine I pointed to it. "Cossacks," the commandant said and I nodded. The commandant left the room and came back with three other officers. I thought we were going to be executed but he told us to "*allez*" and even opened the gate for us.'

The epic escape ended with a trek over the Pyrenees, the feet of the three men bleeding so badly that they were wrapped in napkins. As Kennedy concluded his story and the train began to descend the hill to its terminus, the seaport, Alice had decided that he really was a most attractive man.

'How long is your leave?' she asked the hero.

'Two weeks. I want to get back and get my hands on these bastards. I was drinking in a bar on the Broomielaw last night when the raid on Clydeside began and I went along to see what I could do. They needed strong men to lift the walls and rafters off those who were crying for help. I've got a lot of scores to settle with the Hun. Anyway, Archie here has got himself a very beautiful wife, the lucky bugger. If you ever tire of him, you know who to come to.'

The following week, after she had settled on her first married home on the seafront, Alice received a letter from Neenie: 'The canary that Willie brought home from Clydebank never sang for us and it died this morning. Willie buried it at the back of the tenement.'

On the morning after the bank dinner in St Enoch's Hotel, Archie told his spouse that before meeting Murdo and Marsaili for lunch he wanted to make a sentimental journey to his pre-war haunts in the city. Instead of taking a taxi they walked down Sauchiehall Street.

'I thought the Grand Hotel was here,' Alice said, confused.

'It was,' Archie agreed, and asked a passer-by, to be told that their honeymoon venue had been demolished. They crossed the hazardous street and walked along St George's Road.

'Where's Scotia Street?' the bank manager asks helplessly as they stand watching the traffic roaring past on the different levels of roads.

Alice catches the sleeve of a passer-by and shouts the name above the racket. The old man puts his trembling mouth close to her ear: 'They pulled the area down to make way for that bloody motorway! I was born in Shamrock Street, but most of it's gone too.'

Archie stands there, holding on to his wide-brimmed homburg in case the slipstream of the traffic carries it away. He's trying to work out where Scotia Street was, but is disorientated. Is that articulated lorry roaring through where the tenement stood, the second floor flat a place of laughter, *sgeulachdan*, the simple fare of potatoes and herring eaten with the fingers from newspapers, Neenie, the *cailleach*, Willie the policeman telling of his latest encounter with keelies, the Italian tenor's voice soaring in an aria?

Alice sees that he's crying as he turns away from the relentless rush.